Three of A Kind

SUSAN HAYES

When the chips are down and the stakes are high,
winning takes three of a kind

Dr. Alyson Jefferies treats everyone who comes through the doors of her medical clinic, regardless of species or social standing. The corporations who run the Drift don't approve of her open-door policy, but Alyson is determined to fight for her patients, no matter what.

Cyborg brothers Dirk, Blade, and Lance Trello were designed for combat, but the Resource Wars ended before they drew their first breath. Soldiers without a war, they drift from place to place, looking for a purpose and a reason to settle down.

When corporate secrets and hidden agendas put Alyson's life in peril, the three hot-blooded brothers know they've found a cause worth fighting for. They are going to protect their defiant doctor—while trying to convince her that sometimes the best things in life come in threes.

COPYRIGHT

Three of a Kind
Author: Susan Hayes

ALL RIGHTS RESERVED: This literary work may not be reproduced or transmitted in any form or by any means, including electronic or photographic reproduction, in whole or in part, without express written permission.

All characters and events in this book are fictitious. Any resemblance to actual persons living or dead is strictly coincidental. It is fiction so facts and events may not be accurate except to the current world the book takes place in.

DEDICATION

For my Mum and Dad, for supporting me even when they thought I was crazy. And for my best friend, Karen, for putting up with me when I was definitely nuts.

This book is also dedicated to Violet V. and to Z and S. They know why.

Table of Contents

PROLOGUE

Out on the edge of civilized space lies a rag-tag collection of space stations and platforms known as the Drift. It's a haven for the hunted, the lost, and those seeking second chances. The ones who live there hail from every species, class, and corner of the galaxy, but they all have one thing in common: they don't belong anywhere else.

There's nothing beyond the Drift but wild space and an asteroid belt full of ore-rich rocks. Hundreds of mining vessels and their hard-working crews mine the asteroids. When the ships deliver their haul to be processed, those crews hit the infamous bars, casinos, and pleasure houses that are the Drift's primary source of income…and the only source of entertainment.

It's a world of its own. One where corporations rule, the laws are flexible, and everything is for sale, for the right price.

Welcome to the Drift.

CHAPTER ONE

Dr. Alyson Jefferies was having the kind of day that made her question her career choices. She'd become a doctor to help people, and she had chosen to come to the Drift because she wanted a challenge. Today, her greatest challenge was staying on her feet with minimal sleep and a steady stream of patients who were mostly victims of their own stupidity. Two bar brawls that got out of hand, a miner on shore leave who got stabbed when he was caught cheating at cards, and a freighter pilot who overdosed on *crimson*. The dangerous drug was slowly disappearing from the Drift now that the cartel trafficking it had been broken up, but there were still a few vials around. With all the deaths it had caused, it amazed her that anyone was willing to risk their lives by taking the stuff, but they were still seeing at least one overdose a week.

She trudged to the small staff room and filled a mug with coffee so strong it could be used as rocket fuel before heading to her office. She had reports to write and several orders to check up on, including two shipments of supplies that had gone mysteriously missing and another that had somehow been re-routed to the far side of the galaxy. She was running short of everything from healing accelerants to basic bandages. The corporations that owned the Drift and almost everything and everyone here were sending her a message, making it clear that while she didn't answer to them directly, they were still in control. At least, they thought they were.

As annoying as the shortages were, Alyson was actually relieved by the petty power plays. The corporations had made it clear they didn't like her working on the cyborgs that had once been their property. They were trying to protect their secrets, which was understandable. Having recently uncovered some of those secrets, Alyson now knew the corporations were right to be worried. They had done some despicable things to the cyborgs. Some of it was on the record, but much of what they'd done was still a carefully guarded secret. If they were sticking to cheap tricks like diverting shipments and short-changing her orders, then they didn't know her end goal was to reveal the rest of their dirty laundry to the cosmos. If they figured out what she was up to, then they wouldn't rest until she, and everyone she was working with, were silenced forever.

She dropped into her chair and plunked her mug down on the desk, right beside an identical mug half full of hours-old, cold coffee. There were days she had an entire collection of half-drunk coffees by the end of a shift, and today was looking to be one of them.

She took a moment to refasten her long, blonde hair back into a simple ponytail and then closed her eyes and sent up a prayer to the universe at large. "Just let me have five minutes of peace and quiet. That's all I need."

There was no response, only blessed silence. For the first time in hours, she was alone. No decisions to make. No life and death judgments. She exhaled slowly, willing her mind and body to slow down for a few brief moments of rest. It was all she was likely to get until Dr. Basque's shift started in a couple of hours.

Five minutes later, she opened her eyes and tried to convince herself she felt more alert and ready to tackle the backlog of paperwork waiting for her. That's when she saw it - a perfectly folded paper pyramid sitting on top of a stack of files in the middle of her desk. It was less than three inches across, made of blood red paper, and it hadn't been there the last time she'd sat down.

It was only a piece of paper, but something about it made her feel uneasy. The color, maybe. Or the fact that it had suddenly appeared inside her locked office. "Or, I could be overreacting to absolutely nothing because I'm over-caffeinated. Get a grip, Alyson. It's just a piece of paper... And now I'm talking to myself, too. *Fraxxing* perfect. "

She picked up the intricately folded object, taking a moment to note the crisp lines and perfect symmetry of the piece. Precision like this took time. Whoever had made this, they hadn't done it quickly. When she turned it over, she saw two words written on the bottom in black ink. "Open me."

She unfolded it with care, and though her hands were steady, her pulse was galloping by the time she managed to undo the intricate twists and creases. She smoothed out on the desktop and read the short note written inside.

You're in grave danger. Protect yourself, or you won't live to finish what you've started.

"Cryptic and ominous. Wonderful." She turned the paper over, looking for something—anything—more, but that was all there was. No name. No explanation. No hint as to what the danger was, or how to protect herself.

So much for her theory that the petty inconveniences indicated the corporations didn't know what she was up to. *Somebody* had figured it out. She stared at the note, wishing there was more to it. Which of the corporations was after her? Who had written the warning, and how the hell had they gotten in and out of her office without being seen?

Security at the med center had always been good, but in the last few weeks, the entire system had been upgraded to the point she felt ridiculously over-protected. At least she *had*. Until now. "Computer, call up all security footage for the corridor outside my office for the last three hours. Scan and identify everyone who appears."

Less than a minute later she was staring at a list of everyone who had come and gone from the area around her door. There were no surprises. Herself, several members of the staff, including Anne, their receptionist, and several patients had passed by, but no one else.

"Alright. Let's try a different approach. Computer, display a list of all the times my office door was opened in the past twelve hours, with timestamps and access codes used."

The air shimmered as the display changed to her new request. It wasn't a long list of entries, and at first, everything looked exactly the way she expected. The only access code used was hers. She checked the timestamps, ticking them off one by one until she got to the second-last entry. According to the time stamp, the code had been entered while she was at the other end of the med-center, stitching up the would-be card shark. Someone had gotten in without being seen, and they'd used her code to do it.

Her unease elevated into something closer to fear. If she couldn't stop this mysterious someone from getting into her highly secured office, how the *fraxx* was she supposed to protect herself from whoever or whatever was coming for her?

"Computer. Display security footage of corridor outside my office for timestamp thirteen hundred hours, thirty-seven minutes, eight seconds." Though the computer hadn't detected anyone in the corridor, there had to be someone there. The door hadn't opened on its own.

She watched intently, her fatigue temporarily banished by adrenaline. She didn't see anything on the first pass. No one so much as paused outside her door. "Computer. Rewind to the same timestamp and play again at one-quarter speed."

This time, she saw something. A shimmer in the air outside her door. Even now, it would have been easy to dismiss it as a trick of the light. It wasn't.

"Got you." She froze the image and stared at it, but no matter how long she looked, she couldn't make out anything except that the distortion was more or less human-shaped. She was about to zoom in for a better look when her comm device erupted in a familiar sequence of chirps and beeps.

She answered the call with a touch of her hand. "What's coming in, Anne?

"There's been an accident on board one of the ore refinery ships. The patient was repairing one of the machines and it re-activated. Crush injury to right hand and forearm. ETA is seven minutes. You're going to want Lieksa on this one."

"Patient's a cyborg?"

Anne hesitated a second before confirming. "It's Nya."

Damn it.

She locked down her emotions and cleared her mind. Nya needed her to be a doctor right now, not a friend. "I'll be right out. Tell Lieksa to meet me in O.R. Two. I'll brief her before Nya gets here."

Nya was already one of Alyson's patients. In fact, as one of the few cyborg females on the Drift, she was part of Alyson's research project. By examining her and several others, Alyson had determined that the women had all been exposed to a substance that rendered them infertile. Now, she was working on a cure. When it was done, Nya would be one of the first to receive it.

Alyson took a quick swig of her coffee and then raced to the surgical suite. Lieksa Kiv was possibly the only person on the Drift who could repair Nya's cybernetic implants. There was no one more qualified, but Nya had never met the former lab tech, and she wasn't the kind to trust easily. Like most cyborgs, Nya had little reason to trust the corporations or the techs who worked for them, and until a few weeks ago, Lieksa had been a corporate employee.

The mystery of her cryptic note and the blur outside her door would have to wait. Nya needed her right now, and the needs of her patients always came first.

* * * *

Dirk Trello had his back to the showers, but he didn't need to see to know the second his brothers finally joined him in the Corp-Sec locker room. They were making more noise than a herd of

Nantari rhinos in mating season; laughing, joking, and insulting each other with every breath.

He turned to face them. "Move your asses, or we're going to be late. I don't understand how the *fraxx* we can be identical triplets when only one of us understands the concept of being on time."

"It's one of the mysteries of the universe. Like trying to explain why we all came out of the maturation tank at the same time, and yet you have always acted like you're the oldest and therefore the one in charge," Blade shot back. He deliberately shook his head, sending a spray of water splattering across Dirk's dry shirt.

"Someone has to be," Dirk said, and both his brothers chimed in, reciting the phrase beat for beat with him.

"See, we're clearly related," Lance said.

"And yet, I'm the only one dressed."

"You're grumpy today. Nervous about seeing the doc or something?" Blade asked.

"We're not seeing her. Lieksa's doing the procedure. She said it won't take more than a couple of minutes. We'll be in and out so quick the doc won't even know we've been there."

"Then why are you so twitchy? Lieksa isn't going to care if we're a few minutes late."

"She won't care, but her boyfriends will. They're taking her out tonight, and I got an earful from Mack about making sure she got out of there on time."

Lance chuckled. "Gotcha. No pissing off the new bosses. That, I can understand. You should have said something sooner."

"Must have slipped my mind." It didn't matter that they were going to see Lieksa and not Dr. Jefferies, thoughts of the willowy blonde doctor had distracted Dirk all day. He'd never wanted a woman the way he wanted her, and she wasn't interested. The more they flirted, the harder she pushed them away. It was a losing game, but one neither he nor his brothers could seem to stop playing.

"Told you, it's the good doctor. She's messing with your head, Dirk." Blade said.

"Like you're any better." Lance reached out to tug on Blade's long hair, tied back into a ponytail instead of loose like he usually wore it. "This is a new look for you. Trying to look slightly less disreputable, are we? Might I suggest trimming your beard, too? You're a mess, man."

"Shut up." Blade swatted Lance's hand away. "Nice shirt, by the way. That's new."

"Shut up, yourself. I liked the color, that's all. The clerk at the store said it's the same shade as my eyes." Lance smoothed a hand over the dark green fabric.

Blade opened his mouth to make a retort, but Dirk cut him off. "Okay, so we're clearly all having the same issue – Dr. Alyson Jefferies. Glad we got that cleared up. Can we go now?"

"*Fraxx*, yes. Before we start talking about our feelings or something." Blade closed the door of his locker and grinned. "Have I mentioned how much I love this new job? Good pay, nice job perks, and they've even got our names on our lockers. It's the little things in life that make all the difference."

"I've heard little things are good for amusing little minds," Lance said, and the two of them were off on another round of insults.

At least this time they were walking while they did it. It didn't matter if they were seeing Alyson today or not, he was determined to be on time. Manners weren't programmed into their behavior protocols, and it certainly wasn't a skill they needed on long-haul freighters, mining ships, or other odd jobs they'd worked for the last eighteen months. It *was* something they needed if they were going to get Alyson's attention, though.

Fortunately, Corp-Sec headquarters wasn't far from the med-center. They made it with seconds to spare, despite the heavy throng of off-duty workers and mining crews on shore leave that filled the space station's main causeway. If the early crowd was any indication, the next shift at Corp-Sec was going to be a busy one when the newly freed crews starting enjoying themselves in earnest. Thankfully, they were off work until tomorrow. Tonight's trouble was someone else's problem.

The waiting area was empty, but judging from the weary expression on Anne's face, it hadn't been a quiet day. "Hey, Anne. We're here to see Lieksa about getting a new comms channel activated."

"Technician Kiv is unavailable. A cyborg came in an hour ago with a nasty crush injury, and Lieksa is repairing her implants. You can reschedule, or…" Anne trailed off as she checked something on her screen. For a moment, her lips curved up into a mischievous grin, but when she looked up again, her features were carefully schooled once more. "As it happens, Dr. Jefferies is free right now. She's done this procedure before. Would you mind seeing her, instead?"

"We wouldn't mind at all."

None of them had ever had to chase a woman before. It was fun, at least at first. Lately, it had been more frustrating than enjoyable. They wanted Alyson, and none of them had any idea how to make that happen. If Anne was willing to help them out, then they'd happily accept the favor.

Anne nodded, and he caught another glimmer of a smile. "I'll let her know. If you would follow me, I'll take you to your room, and you can get settled. Do you know which of you is going first?"

"That would be me," Blade said. Blade was always the one charging in first. He volunteered for the most dangerous assignments, took the toughest jobs, and stood between the world and his brothers, protecting them as best he could. This should be a simple procedure, but none of them had been to see a lab-tech since the day they were freed. This was unknown territory for all of them.

Anne left them in one of the nondescript rooms of the med-center. The second the door slid shut, Dirk turned to Blade. "Don't screw this up for us. No flirting. No innuendoes, and try to be a gentleman."

Blade snorted with laughter. "None of us know how to behave that way."

Lance chimed in. "It's easy, Blade. Just do the exact opposite of your first instincts, and you should be fine."

"Asshole," Blade shot back.

"I rest my case. Next time, drop the locker room insults and try to be charming, instead."

Dirk slapped his open hand against an open stretch of countertop, making everything sitting on it rattle and jump. "This is what I'm talking about. It's time we stepped up our game. I don't want to be drifting around the galaxy alone for the rest of my life, and I know you don't, either."

His brothers quieted and then nodded in unison. Dirk nodded with them. Despite being genetically identical, they didn't always agree on everything. When they did, though, there wasn't a force in the universe that could stop them.

CHAPTER TWO

Alyson exited the surgical suite feeling hopeful. Nya's injuries weren't as bad as she had feared, and the wounded cyborg had accepted Lieksa's help with only minimal resistance.

"Everything going well in there?" Anne was waiting for her in the corridor with a fresh mug of coffee in her hand. Since Anne only drank tea, that could only mean one thing: there were other patients waiting. The coffee was a peace offering and a sure sign that she wasn't going to get back to her office anytime soon.

She took the offered mug and downed a scalding mouthful before answering. "Better than I hoped, to be honest. Nya should be at one-hundred percent in a matter of days. At least, that's what Lieksa told me. I'm just glad she's working here, now. I still have a lot to learn before I'm half as good as she is with cybernetic implants."

"Fate puts us all where we need to be when we need to be there."

"Mmhmm. And where does Fate think I need to be right at the moment?" She jiggled the mug in her hand. "You wouldn't be bringing me coffee if I didn't have someplace I needed to be."

Anne chuckled. "Very true. You're needed in exam room three. Cyborg patient. A routine comm-channel activation. Lieksa was supposed to do it, but since she's busy, you're up."

"There was a time when I never imagined that anything to do with the cyborgs would be considered routine. Do we have the specs on what needs to be done?"

Anne looked faintly insulted. "Of course we do. Everything you need to know is in the file I just sent you."

"Thank you." She offered Anne a tired smile. "I mean it. You're the glue that holds this place together."

"It's my pleasure, Dr. Jefferies. You take care of everyone else, and I'll do my best to take care of you and the other doctors." She patted Alyson on the cheek. "At least until you find someone better-looking to take over the job."

"There isn't a man in existence foolish enough to take me on, so I think you're going to have a job for life."

Anne clucked and shook her gray head. "The only fools are the ones who can't see what a catch you are. If I had a son your age..."

"They'd be married already, just like the rest of your brood. Aren't seven grandchildren enough for you?" Alyson took one last sip of coffee, took her leave of Anne, and set off for exam room three.

She paused at the door to check the file and frowned when she noticed Anne hadn't included the patient's name. Odd. That wasn't the kind of detail Anne normally missed. Her eyes were still on the file as she entered the room, but she didn't need to look up to know who was waiting for her. No one else in the whole in the galaxy affected her the way the Trello triplets did.

The tablet slipped a little in her hand, and she uttered a soft gasp of surprise before she managed to regain her composure. They had to think she was a complete idiot, because every time she met them her normally sharp mind turned to mush and started leaking out her ears. It was embarrassing, but nothing she had tried made it stop.

When she was around the brothers, her carefully crafted armor always seemed to melt away, leaving her feeling vulnerable and slightly off-balance. She hated feeling like that, so invariably she would find some reason to be anywhere the three of them weren't. They made her think of things she was better off without. Dating and love were wonderful concepts in theory, but in her experience, they only led to disappointment and hurt.

"Hello, you three. You startled me." She lifted the tablet, managing to tighten her grip on it at the same time. "Your names weren't on the file I was given. Which of you is here for the comm channel link?"

"Hello, Dr. Jefferies." Dirk spoke first.

She knew it was Dirk, because he was the only one of the three who wore his hair short. She could tell Lance and Blade apart, too. They were physically identical, but they each had their own unique personality and mannerisms.

"Hi," Lance chimed in with an easy, welcoming grin that gave away his identity.

"Hey, Doc. I'm going first, but all three of us are here for the same thing." Blade stepped forward and smiled down at her, eyes twinkling. "We're putting ourselves in your talented hands."

She dove behind the walls of her professional reserve and tried to ignore the pulse-pounding effects of his smile. They were all incredibly attractive, but there was something about Blade's flirtatious smile that made her toes curl. "You have nothing to worry about. I've done several of these procedures, and it's quick and painless."

"You don't have to rush on our account, Doc."

Dirk cleared his throat. "What Blade meant to say was that we appreciate you doing this for us. I know Lieksa was called away to an emergency. Is everything alright with her and her patient?"

Dirk's phrasing seemed stilted, and Alyson wondered if he had misgivings about her stepping in for Lieksa. "She's still finishing up with her patient, but everything looks good. If you'd rather, I could reschedule you for another time when Lieksa is free? I know she's the certified tech, so if you'd prefer—

"Oh, hell, no. We want you," Blade declared.

A jolt of pure need slammed into her, knocking every sane thought out of her head. "You've got me."

"Not yet, we don't," Lance muttered.

"What do you need us to do, Alyson?" Dirk interjected, steering the conversation away from…she wasn't sure what.

What did she need them to do? That was a loaded question. She needed them to stop being so damned attractive, for starters. She didn't have time for distractions, and the Trello brothers had been a source of constant distraction since they'd walked into her life and tried to take over.

"I need Blade to take a seat in that chair over there while I get the equipment. Oh, and you might want to take off your shirt, too. I have to put some contact gel on your skin, and I don't want to ruin your clothing."

Blade grinned. "Strip. Sit. Stay. I can do that."

She turned her back to Blade to give him a bit of privacy, only to find herself face to face with Dirk. "I need to put this down on the counter," she said, holding up her half-drunk cup of coffee and nodding to the countertop behind him.

Instead of moving out of her way, he held out his hand. "I'll take it."

"Thank you." She handed him the mug and tried not to notice the way his fingers brushed against hers as he took it from her. Why was it that the slightest touch or word from any of the brothers did more for her than a night of dinner and dancing with any other man she'd ever met? And why had the universe sent the brothers into her orbit now, of all times? Too many people were counting on her. The cyborgs, her patients, and the other doctors employed at the center. She couldn't take the chance right now.

"Anytime. Anything you need," Dirk said, his vivid green eyes locking with hers.

For a split second, she considered telling him about the note and it's cryptic warning, but she knew it was a bad idea. They were already protective of her. More so than they had any right to be. They had been assigned to guard her clinic and one of her patients last month, and then watched over her for days afterward because they were worried about her visits from corporate lawyers rattling sabers. If they knew she was in real danger, they wouldn't let her out of their sight. They'd turn her life and her med-center upside down and make it impossible for her to accomplish everything she needed to.

"That's sweet of you, but I'm fine. Everything is progressing, if a little slower than I'd like."

Dirk nodded. He and his siblings were all part of the group working to counter corporate interference in the cyborgs' lives. "It's hard to find the answers to questions you can't come out and ask directly, but we're getting there." He grinned. "Slowly."

"I'm not a fan of slow. I understand it's necessary sometimes, but that doesn't mean I have to like it," Blade said.

Once again, Alyson wondered if they were talking about the same thing. Everything the brothers did and said seemed to carry a double meaning. She couldn't decide if it was actually happening, or if her attraction to them affected her thinking. Given the kind of men they were, it was probably both.

"Well, I can promise this will be over quickly. You'll all be out of here in fifteen minutes or so." She turned to face Blade once more. He was seated in the chair as directed, his shirt laid across one thick thigh. It was the first time she'd seen any of them shirtless, and two things struck her right away. The first was that Blade was huge– heavily muscled, with broad shoulders and a build as powerful as it was beautiful. The second thing that hit her was his lack of scars. Every cyborg she had ever treated had them--remnants of injuries not even their nanotech-enhanced bodies could heal perfectly.

"So, how does this work?" Blade asked, watching her intently as she organized the equipment on her tray and carried it over to his side.

"I'll put a little of this gel on your neck and then move this device over your neck until it makes contact with the receiver implanted under your skin. Once they're connected, all I have to do is input the new codes, and you should be linked. I'll have you test it and make sure it's working, and you'll be done." She paused, then added. "Haven't any of you done this before? I thought it was a pretty common procedure."

Blade shook his head. "This is a first for us. We've only ever been able to communicate with each other."

"What about the rest of your batch siblings? Command channels? Surely you had those?"

Lance's answer surprised her. "We were never in combat, Doc. We weren't brought online until after the war was over. It's only ever been the three of us."

"That explains the lack of scars. I was wondering." There were dozens of questions she wanted to ask, but she didn't. None of the cyborgs she'd met liked to talk about their past. There was too much darkness there, and more pain than any doctor could ever hope to heal.

*

Blade tugged at the shirt in his lap, pulling it over the steel rod that had replaced his dick the instant Alyson had told him to take his shirt off. Any second now, she was going to be touching him, and he hoped like hell his cock didn't break the clasp on his pants when she did.

"If you're curious about anything, just ask. My life's an open book, and a short one at that," he told her.

She hesitated for a second and then nodded. "Alright. What's it like, being connected all the time? And are you sure you want to do this, adding more people to your comms? Isn't it going to be a bit invasive to have someone new in your head?"

"We're triplets, which means we're genetically identical. Not to mention we had the same basic behavioral programming installed. We're connected by more than our internal comm channels. It's hard to explain, but most of the time we don't need to talk to each other to know what we're thinking."

She squeezed some of the gel onto her slender fingers, and moved behind him, out of his sight.

"I'm going to apply the gel now. It's going to feel cold."

"You do what you need to, Doc." He could use a little cold right now. Like maybe an entire bucket of ice water dumped over his head. His brothers were both aware of his current problem, and the only reason the bastards weren't laughing out loud was because they knew their turns were coming.

Her gel coated fingers glided over his neck, and his next breath came out in a strangled hiss. Blade had dreamed about having her hands on him since the day they'd met, and now that it was happening, it wasn't enough. He didn't want a gentle, clinical touch. He wanted her stroking him, caressing and exploring. He wanted to span her slender waist in his hands and feel those long legs of hers wrapped around his hips.

"Sorry, the cold sensation will pass in a second," she murmured.

"No problem." Nope, the tiny chill from the gel wasn't his problem. It was the fire in his blood that was going to kill him. Spontaneous combustion due to sexual frustration was not the way he planned to die, but right now, it was a serious possibility.

"I'm going to search for the receiver now. You might feel a slight buzz or itch when it connects. Try not to move if that happens. You ready?"

He started to nod but stopped as he remembered he was supposed to stay still. "Ready."

It only took a few seconds for her to find the receiver and make the connection. There was a momentary tingle, just like she had warned him.

"I'm adding the new codes now. You should be able to talk to Mack and Dash once I'm done. This is their shared comms code, right?"

"Yeah, it's Mack and Dash we're linking with. We report to them on the job, so it made sense. We'll probably link with the others later, but we're taking it slowly." Dirk shrugged. "Like Lance said, this is the first time we've been linked to anyone but ourselves. It's going to take some getting used to."

"This isn't really a Corp-Sec thing though, is it?" she asked.

"Not really. It's another safety measure. We can call each other faster this way, and stay in contact without anyone listening in. With what's going on right now, we need all the protection we can get."

"All of us," Lance agreed. "Most especially the only doctor on the Drift who cares about our kind. You're careful, aren't you, Doc?"

Blade felt the tiny tremors pass from her hand into the receiver pressed to his neck and knew the truth before she even opened her mouth to answer.

"I've got a new security system protecting this place and everyone in it. I'll be fine."

Alyson was lying. Blade was certain of it. Something had their lovely doctor worried, but she was too stubborn to admit it.

"If it wasn't fine, would you tell us?" he asked.

There was a brief pause before she answered, and he swore her fingers trembled again. "If there was anything wrong and I thought you could help, then yes, I'd tell you. But there isn't."

She was lying again. Blade bit his tongue to stop from calling her on it. He didn't know her well enough to know why she was lying, but he did know that if he pushed her, she'd push back hard. If that happened, they'd lose whatever progress they had made with her. The woman was as stubborn as she was beautiful.

"There. You're all set. Try communicating with Mack and Dash, and we'll find out if it worked."

"I've got faith in you, Doc." It took him a second or two to focus enough to activate the link for the first time.

"Hey, guys. Did it work?" he sent the message and got an immediate response.

"It did. Which one are you?" Mack sent back.

"It's Blade. I guess we better learn to introduce ourselves at the beginning of any conversation and save you two the confusion."

"You don't do that for each other?" Dash asked.

"Nope. We can tell each other apart most of the time."

"Did it work?" Alyson asked.

"Perfectly."

"Signing off for now. Time for the doc to link my brothers in."

"Tell her we say hi, and to send Lieksa home once she's done with her patient. We want our girl home." Mack said.

"You got it."

"Mack and Dash say hi, and wanted me to remind you that they want their girlfriend back as soon as possible."

"Of course they do. They get twitchy if she's out of their sight for too long. Are all cyborgs programmed to be overprotective, or is it just the ones I know?"

Lance answered first, and his response was better than anything Blade would have come up with.

"We're all hardwired to defend the things we care about. The corporations programmed us to protect our creators. Once that coding was was removed, the drive to defend and protect was still there, but we can choose what, or who, we care about."

Alyson's only response was a noncommittal hum as she wiped the gel from the back of Blade's neck, then touched a hand to his shoulder. "You're all done. Lance, Dirk, which one of you is next?"

Blade stood, keeping his back to her as he pulled his shirt back on and tugged it down so it hid his erection. He wanted to know what Alyson wasn't telling them, but she already refused to take them seriously, and there was no point in giving her another reason to push them away.

He moved to an unoccupied corner of the room and leaned against the wall as Lance stripped off his shirt and sat down. Alyson went through the same process as before, though it went faster, now that she knew where the implant was. In less than ten minutes, the procedures were over.

"Thank you, Dr. Jefferies. We appreciate you doing this for us today," Dirk said.

"You're welcome. It means a lot that you trusted me to treat you. Especially since this was the first time you had something like this done."

"There's no one we trust more than you," Lance said.

"No one," Blade and Dirk confirmed, speaking at the same time.

Pink spots bloomed on Alyson's cheeks, and her gray eyes brightened to the color of newly minted steel. "Thank you."

For the first time in his life, Blade was struck speechless. Alyson's beauty had captured his interest from the beginning, and he was drawn to her fire like an asteroid caught in a star's gravitational field, but this was the first time he had seen her softer side. A hint of blush, the shine in her eyes, the shy smile that barely touched the corners of her mouth. She took his breath away.

"When do you get off shift, tonight?" The words were out of Blade's mouth before he even knew he was going to speak.

Alyson's guard was back up within seconds. "Officially, another hour. Unofficially, I'll probably be working through the night. I've got a ton of paperwork to catch up on, and I need to touch base with an old friend and find out if she's made any progress tracking down the source of the genetic material the cyborgs were created from."

Blade had planned on asking her to join them for a drink, but it was clear she wasn't going to give him an opening. Instead, he let her change the subject.

"You know a genetic expert?" he asked.

"Not exactly. I know someone who specializes in retrieving digital information and loves a challenge."

Lance chuckled. "How did a nice girl like you cross paths with a cyber jockey? That is what you're talking about, right?"

"Phaedra and I were roommates back in college. She dropped out eventually, but we stayed in touch. She's the only person I know who could track down the information we're after and retrieve it without getting caught."

"She must be good," Dirk said.

"She's one of the best."

No one knew where the DNA used to create the cyborgs had come from. That information was buried deep in the corporations' vaults along with almost everything else known about the cyborg design and creation process. The corporations might have been forced to free their creations, but they would never give up the secret of how they were made.

Alyson glanced to toward the door. "I've got other patients waiting for me, and I should relay the message to Lieksa that her guys are waiting for her at home."

They were being dismissed.

"We'll talk outside and make a plan. This isn't over." Dirk said over their internal comm channel.

"Damn right, it's not. She's lying to us. Something's wrong." Blade replied.

"Cool your boosters. We'll talk about it outside," Lance shot back.

They said their goodbyes and left the med center, though he lingered in the hall long enough to see Alyson vanish into her office. Now he knew where to find her when he came back. And he had every intention of coming back, whether his brothers approved of the plan or not.

The main concourse of Astek space station was still full of beings from every species and corner of the galaxy, but everyone was walking with purpose. Astek was primarily a recreation platform, offering a host of pleasures and entertainments to the miners and workers who called the Drift home. Most of the crowd was looking for their next distraction and headed for the flashing lights and raucous noise that flowed out of the clubs further down the causeway.

Blade and his brothers claimed an empty bench across from the medical center. The second they were seated, Blade turned to the others. "So, what's our next move?"

"One of us needs to talk to her and tell her we're concerned something's going on. She might not want our help, but she has to accept *someone's* help. No one can do it all alone." Lance bumped his fist into Dirk's shoulder. "We've got each other, but Alyson is determined to do this on her own."

"She hasn't taken the boost Zale offered her, either," Dirk said.

He was referring to the medi-bots all cyborgs carried. When Zale had joined their small cadre of rebels, the big half-Torski had revealed that he was one of the experts who originally created the microscopic technology. He had offered the human members of the group access to a modified version of the medi-bots which would give them accelerated healing, exceptional longevity, and a lifetime of near perfect health.

"You can't be sure," Lance said.

"Yeah, we can. She looked tired, and when she came into the room she was carrying a fresh mug of coffee. She wouldn't need caffeine to stay on her feet if she were uh, boosted." Blade drummed his fingers against his thigh. "I want to go back and talk to her about all of this."

Dirk folded his arms over his chest. "The line forms behind me."

"If we all go marching in there together, she's going to shut down and deny anything is wrong. Since we all want to do it, there's only one solution." Lance held out his hand in a loose fist. "Best two out of three gets to go."

Blade groaned. "I hate this *fraxxing* game. Why do we make decisions this way?"

"Because beating each other up takes too long and draws too much attention."

"Yeah, but it's a lot more fun." Blade looked at Dirk. "You taking on the winner of round one?"

"I still don't see how a piece of paper can possibly win against a chunk of rock. It's illogical," Dirk grumbled. "Yeah, I've got dibs on the winner. Once I beat them, I'll go talk to Alyson."

"Good luck." Blade touched his fist to Lance's. Rock, paper, scissors wasn't the most adult way to decide matters, but it worked.

CHAPTER THREE

Alyson sat at her desk and stared at the security footage projected over her desk. She had been staring at the blurred shape for the last five minutes, and she still had no better understanding of who it could be or how they had gotten her access codes. She had never felt so vulnerable. It was an unsettling sensation. She had managed to push the matter aside while she was busy working, but now she was back in her office she couldn't shake a sense of foreboding. Her office wasn't a sanctuary anymore.

Doubts nagged her. Maybe she should have told Dirk, Lance, and Blade what was going on. Their kind of help would be disruptive to everything she was doing, but was that a reasonable justification for lying to them?

She pinched the bridge of her nose and uttered a low groan of frustration. She already knew the answer. Her lie had less to do with any possible disruption, and everything to do with her attraction to the brothers. She was pushing them away because she was afraid of what would happen if she let them get too close. That excuse didn't hold up as well now there was a greater threat.

"I've got too much on my plate already, and now I've got you lurking around, leaving me cryptic, threatening messages, you blurry bastard!" Frustrated, she hurled a stylus through the floating image at the same moment the door opened.

Lance caught the pen flying straight at his face. "Whoa. Okay, next time I'll knock first."

"Yes, knocking would be good. You know what else would be great? Telling me how you opened my office door without a passcode."

Lance winked at her. "But I do have one."

"No, you couldn't have. The security system is brand new."

"Then whoever installed it copied over the passcodes from the old system, including the one Corp-Sec gave to us when we were assigned to guard this place." He frowned. "Which means you're not as secure as you thought."

"Apparently not. You still shouldn't have walked in without knocking. What if I was with a patient?"

"I checked with Anne. She said you were in your office alone." He arched a dark brow at her. "Do you often talk to yourself and throw things when you're alone?"

"Only when I'm as frustrated as I am at the moment." She waved him inside. "Is there something I can do for you? You only left a few minutes ago."

He moved into the room, and the door slid shut behind him. "I'm here because we know you weren't entirely honest with us before. We're worried about you, Alyson." His gaze fell on the security footage still projected above her desk. "Is that guy shielded? Where was this taken? When?"

"Shielded? What are you talking about?"

Lance pointed to the image. "I'm talking about that, right there." His brow furrowed as he read the date stamped at the bottom. "Son of a starbeast, that was taken outside your office door today! What's going on Alyson?"

"I'm not sure."

Lance growled in frustration, and the next thing she knew he was leaning over her, his hands gripping the arms of her chair to cage her in. His green eyes were narrowed in frustration, and she could actually hear the chair creak in protest of the abuse he was inflicting with his grip.

"Is that what you didn't want to tell us about before? Did someone sneak into the med center? Did he hurt you?"

"This is why I didn't tell you. I knew you'd overreact. Well, to be honest, I thought it would be Blade or Dirk who'd go caveman first, but my point still stands."

His nostrils flared. "If they were here, you would already be over their shoulder while they carried you somewhere safe. Like the bunkers below Corp-Sec HQ. Since I'm supposed to be the nice one, I'm trying to give you a moment to explain before I do that. So, explain. Fast."

"You are definitely not the nice brother."

He chuckled. It was a low rumble that rose up from his chest and washed over her like summer thunder. "The truth is, none of us is the nice one. We weren't made that way. I'm quieter, but that's not because I'm sweet. It's because I'm watching, learning, and waiting to make my move."

She was caged in by the solid bulk of his body, close enough she could feel his body heat and breathe in the subtle notes of sandalwood and citrus that clung to his skin. It was nearly impossible to think, but she managed to find her tongue.

"I'll talk once you back off, mister making-a-move." She shoved at his chest, which was like trying to push on the outer hull of the station and expecting the whole thing to move.

"Nope. I'm not going anywhere until you tell me what the *fraxx* is going on."

"Someone was in my office today. They used my new security code, came in, left me a note, and left without anyone seeing them. The security system didn't even register their presence. I was trying to figure out who it was, so I called up the footage of the hallway at the time the office door was last opened. That's what's in the image. That's all I know because after that I was called out to an emergency and left my office. I haven't been back in here since."

Lance glanced up at the projection, then lowered his head until he was looking into her eyes. "You should have told us."

"After the way you three turned this place upside down the last time you had guard duty? I have too many people depending on me right now. There's too much I need to do." Even as she said the words, she heard how weak they sounded.

"And you can't do any of it if you're not here. Now, tell me about the note. What did it say?"

The rest of the story came out in a rush, and relief filled her the second she was done. "It was folded into this perfect little pyramid of red paper. There was a note written inside stating I was in danger and I needed to protect myself or I wouldn't survive."

"And you thought you could deal with that on your own? Dammit, Alyson. What were you thinking?"

"I was thinking that if I told you and your brothers about all this, you were going to turn my life inside out again." She blew out a soft breath before finishing her confession. "And if that happened, I knew I'd end up doing something a lot crazier than taking on the corporations and some unknown threat. In case you haven't noticed, my schedule is rather full right now. I don't really have room for any more insane decisions."

"Yeah, like what?" Lance asked, moving in so close his breath fanned across her face.

Do I dare admit the truth? She hesitated, afraid of what would happen if she uttered the words out loud. In her experience, admitting you cared about someone gave them the power to disappoint you. "Something really stupid, like let myself get involved with three cyborg brothers who aren't good at taking no for an answer."

He cocked his head to one side. "Why would that be a stupid idea? You've probably noticed we're on board. And before you tell me you have too much to do, and too much riding on your shoulders, I'm going to say one thing. You are exhausting yourself taking care of everyone else and making sure they have what they need. That's admirable. Hell, it's part of why I like you so damned much, but the thing is, you don't have anyone taking care of you. Dirk, Blade, and I would like to be the ones to do that."

There was probably a logical counterargument to Lance's offer, but she couldn't think of one. She wasn't really thinking logically at all. If she were, she would have never admitted to any of the things she'd just confessed to. "It's still probably a bad idea. But…"

"But nothing. You're in danger. We want to protect you. Let us. Say yes, Alyson."

"You promise not to turn this place into an armed fortress? I'll still be able to see my patients? All of them, not just the ones you deem safe?"

"I'm not promising any such thing. We'll do whatever we must to protect you. And I'm taking that as a yes."

"But I didn't agree yet." She protested, glaring at him.

"You're negotiating, which means you will agree, eventually. I've already told Dirk and Blade. They're on their way back, which means we have less than a minute before they come through that door."

"You're assuming an awful lot."

"It's part of my charm." He leaned in and brushed a surprisingly tender kiss to her cheek. "We're going to take care of you, sunshine. I promise."

He moved away before she could react to his promise or the kiss. Not that she was sure how to react to either one. All she knew was that at some point in the last few minutes, her life had taken an unexpected turn. Now she was on a new trajectory with no idea where she would wind up, if she even survived the trip.

*

Moving away from Alyson wasn't what Lance wanted to do. He wanted to gather her into his arms and kiss her until she was soft and pliant and had forgotten about all the pressure she was under. It wasn't the time for that, though. Not yet. "Show me the note. You're the only one to touch it, right?

We should keep it that way in case there's DNA or fingerprints or something on it."

"It's on the desk. Do you think there would be fingerprints? That would be a big mistake for someone to make."

"I doubt it, but I don't want Mack and Dash kicking my ass for messing with evidence, so, let's err on the side of caution."

"That's a good idea."

The compliment surprised him. He was used to being dismissed as all brawn, no brains, or even as something less than human. "Thanks."

He barely had time to scan the note before the thunder of boots announced the arrival of his siblings. "We've got incoming. You might want to unlock the door before they start putting dents in it."

"Won't they just use the same code you did?"

He shook his head. "They know someone threatened your life. Do you think they're going to stop to punch in an access code?" If she thought a door would slow them down, then their lovely doctor had a lot to learn. She was in danger, which meant there was nothing in the galaxy that would keep them away. She was too important to the cause, and even more important to the three of them.

"Good point. Computer, activate open door setting."

The footsteps barely slowed as the door opened and Dirk and Blade fought to get through the doorway first. As entrances went, it wasn't ideal, though it certainly demonstrated their enthusiasm.

"Why didn't you tell us someone threatened you?" Blade demanded as he elbowed his way past Dirk.

"Because I thought you'd overreact." Alyson raised a blonde brow. "Like charging down the hallway of a medical center and nearly coming to blows getting through the door. You know, something like that."

Lance snickered. "She has a point, guys. You knew I was with her. Did you really need to charge in like a pair of enraged Torskis?"

"Yes," Dirk replied.

Alyson sighed. "I'm already regretting this. You can't disrupt the med-center like that. My patients need a safe, quiet place, and the rest of the staff deserve to be able to work in peace. If you can't agree to that, then this isn't going to work."

"We'll make it work," Lance interjected before his brothers could respond. He wasn't sure how the hell he'd become the voice of reason, but if that's what it took to stay close to Alyson then he'd deal with it.

"I see the footage of our suspect, but where's the note?" Blade asked.

Alyson pointed to a dark red piece of paper on her desk. "It's there. But I'm not sure if whoever left it is a suspect, or an ally. Think about it, if he could get in here without being seen, he could have waited for me to come back and attacked. Instead, he left a note warning me to watch my back. That makes him a friend, not a foe. Right?"

Dirk scowled. "Maybe. Maybe not. We don't know enough to make that call. Hell, we can't be sure the figure in the image is a man. I'm not assuming anything right now. All we know for certain is someone got in here and left you a warning."

Lance stayed back with Alyson while his brothers read the note without touching it. There was silence for a while, then Blade looked up. "This bit about finishing what you started. Is there any way that could refer to something besides the cure you're working on?"

She chewed on her lip, then shook her head. "There are a few things it could be, but all of them are related to the cyborgs, and all of them are supposed to be a carefully guarded secret. How could they know about any of it?"

"We'll figure it out." Dirk crossed the room to stand in front of Alyson. "We're going to keep you safe. You're probably not going to love our methods, but anything we do will be for your protection."

"You guarded one of my patients before. I'm familiar with your methods."

Blade joined them. "That was different. This time, we're not guarding a patient in the med-center. We're guarding *you*. That means at least one of us is going to be with you all day, every day until this is dealt with. We're going to make this place as secure as possible, and your home is going to be a *fraxxing* fortress."

"My home and the med-center are one and the same, remember?" She pointed up. "I live one floor up, and the only way to my place is through the med-center. I'll be fine."

"Yeah, you will be, because we'll be up there with you," Lance said.

"In my home?" she asked.

"Mmhmm. I've already contacted Mack. We're being reassigned as your personal security detail. If anyone asks, the official line is that the Drojo Cartel has made threats against you for helping the *crimson* task force shut them down."

"Just like that?" she asked, incredulous.

Blade snapped his fingers. "Presto, we're now your bodyguards."

"I'm starting to think networking you to their comm channel was a bad idea." There wasn't any malice in her words, only resignation. She was finally going to accept their help. It might have taken a death threat to make her give in, but they had a shot at getting to know her, now. And more importantly, she would have time to get to know them. It's all they wanted.

Now, they had to make sure she stayed in one piece long enough for them to sweep her off her feet.

*

Alyson sank into her chair and tried to wrap her head around everything. She had tried to minimize the truth about what the note meant, but she couldn't do that anymore. Somehow, someone knew what she was doing. She didn't know how, but that didn't matter right now. It was a fact, and she had to stop avoiding reality simply because it was inconvenient. The message, and its delivery, were stark reminders that she was vulnerable.

A hand touched her shoulder. "Corp-Sec is sending over forensics to look at the note and someone to take a statement from you. While that happens, we're going to start working on a plan to secure this place. It's going to be alright." Dirk told her.

She exhaled slowly. "I should tell Anne to clear my schedule and call in one of the other doctors to finish my shift. I'm not going to be available for a while, am I?"

"You're done for the day, Doc. Once Corp-Sec clears out, we have to talk about how this is going to work." Dirk gave her a lopsided grin. "I hope your place is bigger than ours because we're going to be staying with you until this is settled."

"My place is more than big enough. That won't be a problem." Her residence was palatial by space station standards. The upper floor was almost as large as the med-center itself. She had converted part of the space into a second office, but there was still plenty of space. She had offered it to the other staff, but all of them had families and preferred to live in the more residential areas of Astek station.

Housing wouldn't be a problem. Having three attractive, overzealous bodyguards in her personal space for the foreseeable future was another matter entirely.

Blade perked up. "More than big enough? We're living in a closet right now. If your place is bigger, I might never leave."

"You can each have your own room, and there's a guest bathroom. I think you'll be comfortable enough."

Lance uttered a low whistle. "Our own rooms? Damn. That'll be a novel experience. We've never had enough scrip to live separately."

Alyson happily seized on the chance to change the subject. "Why wouldn't you have enough? The corporations all provided back pay for your years of service, didn't they?"

Dirk shrugged. "They did. But we didn't come online until it was all over. We didn't qualify for back pay. Astek gave us a small amount of scrip, which was more than they were legally required to do, but that's it. They cut us loose with the rest of the cyborgs, and we've made our own way ever since."

"But that's not right. You didn't get any time to adjust? No training to help?"

"Unlike the rest of our brethren, we woke up with free will. They never activated most of our behavioral programming. We went through a bunch of tests to make sure we were safe to be around other people, and once we passed, they sent us on our way." Blade's tone was light, but his expression belied his easy words.

"At least we were released. We've heard stories that some of the other corporations never woke their last batches at all." Lance shook his head.

"I had no idea. I thought the corporations would have done more for all of you. Given what I've witnessed, I should've known better." Her hand covered her mouth as she remembered something they'd told her the first night they had met. "You named yourselves. I forgot. I didn't realize until now that you had to, because they didn't even give you a name."

"You said whoever named us clearly didn't get enough hugs as a child. You were right. We were never kids, and there were zero snuggles." Blade opened his arms and winked at her. "If ever you feel like helping me up my hug count, I'm game."

She left her chair and went to him, slipping her arms around his waist and giving him a gentle hug. He stiffened in surprise at first, but then he relaxed and uttered a soft, contented sigh. The hug was supposed to be for his benefit, but when his arms closed around her shoulders, she realized she needed the comfort more than he did. She leaned into his strength and closed her eyes.

Blade's hands stroked down her back, and then up to cradle the back of her head, and his fingers tangled in her hair. None of them spoke, and she let the moment stretch longer than she should have. It felt good to lean on someone else for a while. It was a luxury she didn't allow herself very often.

When she pulled back, Blade let her go, but he let his fingers graze her cheek as she stepped away.

"If I had known all I had to do was ask for a hug, I'd have done it weeks ago."

"You caught me in a moment of weakness."

"Weak? Don't sell yourself short, sunshine. You're one of the strongest women I've ever met," Lance said.

She glanced over at him. "That is the second time you've called me sunshine. Is this going to be a thing?"

He grinned. "Don't evade the compliment. And yeah, it's a thing now. It's this, or sweet cheeks. Your choice."

"My choice is that you call me Dr. Jefferies," she replied, folding her arms over her chest.

"Okay, Sunshine it is." Lance chuckled as she glowered at him.

It wasn't fair. She could get even the most difficult patients to sit down and take their medicine with the same look. Eight-foot tall Torski males quailed when she glared at them. So, why was it that when she tried the same thing on Blade, Lance, or Dirk, they laughed?

"I'm not going to win this fight, am I?" she asked.

"No." All three of them answered at once.

She hid her smile. She shouldn't be amused by their antics. They were going to drive her crazy and make everything complicated and chaotic. They were as much a threat to her carefully organized life as whoever was coming after her. Still, she felt better knowing they were here.

She looked at the three towering men who surrounded her and felt her pulse kick up another notch. *Fraxx*. She was in serious trouble.

CHAPTER FOUR

It took longer than Dirk would have liked, but eventually, they got Alyson into the private elevator that was the only access point to the doctor's private quarters. It was a tight fit, but none of them were interested in being left behind.

They had formulated a plan while Alyson had given her statement, and they had stood with her while she let the other doctors and staff know what was happening. They'd met everyone the last time they had been assigned guard duty at the med-center, but she re-introduced them as her private security detail along with the official explanation of why they would be protecting her for the next while. Everyone took it in stride except Anne. The self-appointed mother hen had cursed a blue streak that would make most miners blush, and threatened every member of the Drojo Cartel with slow, painful deaths.

"This elevator seems a lot smaller than normal," Alyson muttered from her spot near the back. "Is it really necessary for all three of you to come with me?"

"Yes, it is. Lance will stay with you while Blade and I sweep your home and make sure there are no surprises waiting."

Speaking of surprises, I should tell you about Huey. He's—"

The door opened, and Dirk stepped out before Alyson finished speaking. Whatever she had to say would have to wait. He was on high alert, scanning for anything out of place. He barely had time to register the dimensions of the room and the placement of the furniture before a voice startled him.

"Good evening, Dr. Jefferies. I was not aware we were having company tonight."

He went on the attack at the first word he heard but pulled up short when he realized who, or rather what, was speaking. Blade didn't slow down. He flew by Dirk and tackled the service droid, taking it down hard enough he heard the pop and snap of parts as it hit the floor.

"Huey!" Alyson stormed into the room, madder than a wet Pheran. "Blade Trello, you did not just break my brand-new droid. He's not a threat to anything but dust bunnies."

"Oops," Blade untangled himself from the droid. "In my defense, you should have mentioned you had a robot running around up here."

Alyson pointed to the damaged droid. "Do shielded assassins normally greet their targets by name and inquire about guests? You did exactly what I was afraid of. Charge in, take over, and cause chaos. If you had just listened to me, I was trying to tell you about Huey in the elevator."

Dirk walked over to Blade and hauled his brother back to his feet. This wasn't an auspicious start to their time with Alyson. "We're sorry about the droid. Right, Blade?"

"Yeah. Sorry." Blade rubbed the back of his neck, looking more than a little sheepish.

"Don't be sorry, do better." Alyson knelt down beside her droid and sighed. "Huey, damage report, please."

"I have sustained damage to several joints, and I appear to have lost my visual sensors. Apologies, Dr. Jefferies. It appears I will be unable to serve you until I am repaired. Would you like me to book myself an appointment?"

"I know someone who should be able to put you to rights, again. Place yourself in standby mode, and I will reactivate you once you're repaired."

"As you wish, Dr. Jefferies. I do apologize for the inconvenience." The droid powered down.

"Where do you want me to put it, uh…him?" Blade asked.

"His recharging station is over in that corner. If you could carefully set Huey on it, I'll call Lieksa and see if she can make a house call."

Blade followed her directions to the letter, and her tension visibly eased once the droid was settled.

"Why is its name Huey?" Blade asked.

"I had to call him something. He's a household unit--H.U. I just tacked another syllable on the end of his name." She swept an arm out to encompass the area. "Welcome to my home. Try not to break anything else, please."

"It won't happen again," Dirk promised. Her home wasn't what he had expected. For one thing, it was larger than he imagined. Living aboard a space station meant that every cubic inch came at a premium. He and his brothers lived in a residential cubby on one of the lower decks, and their entire quarters could fit into the room he was currently standing in.

"Why don't you stay with me while they check out the rest of the place? I can explain what shielding is, and they'll be done by the time I'm done," Lance said.

"Alright. Can I at least sit down, or does my couch pose some threat I'm not aware of?"

"Sit. Relax. It's been a long day." Dirk glared at Blade and sent him a message via their internal comm channel. *"Come on, let's give her some space before she rethinks this arrangement and tosses us out."*

"Don't act so superior. You were about to dismantle the damned thing yourself."

"Yeah, but I stopped. You didn't."

Blade didn't bother to respond. He knew he had screwed up. The two of them split up and started a sweep of the residence, which gave Dirk time to take in the décor and get a glimpse of who Alyson was when she was at home. He had expected sleek, modern furnishings, something elegant, but that wasn't what he saw. The effect was more of a cozy home, with rustic designs that mimicked hewn logs and polished wood. The color scheme was a buttery yellow, with splashes of red and orange. It was a warm, welcoming place. A real home. At least, what he imagined a real home might feel like.

It took a few minutes to ensure that various rooms were empty, but once they were done, he and Blade were certain they were alone. A personal shield generator worked by bouncing light waves so that the one being shielded was more or less invisible. It required a massive amount of power, which meant it could only be operated for short periods. It had limitations, too. It couldn't hide a heat signature very well for one thing, and cyborg senses were too enhanced for them to be fooled by a shield for long.

For the moment, everything was secure, and he intended to see it stayed that way.

Once Dirk was sure they were safe he relaxed a little, and it struck him that, for a little while at least, this warm, cozy place was home. It was a pleasing thought. They returned to the main room in time to hear Lance asking about the full-sized vid screen that took up most of one wall. It was currently displaying a cabin-style wall that matched the furnishings, and through a picture window, there was a snowy vista of a valley floor at twilight.

"It's based on the view out of my grandparent's window back on Cassien Alpha. I don't get home very often, but the view reminds me of them. My grandma made this quilt herself." Alyson reached back to pat the multicolored patchwork blanket resting on the back of the sofa. "She still quilts and knits, and she sends them to me. She keeps telling me that space is cold and I need to stay warm." She sighed. "I need to visit, soon. They're getting older, and I don't want to have regrets once they're gone."

"What's stopping you?" Lance asked.

"Nothing. And everything. I've got to finish the cure first. And we're busy trying to track down the cyborgs that might not have been freed. I'm still tracing the DNA samples that were used to create you, and on top of that, there's the med-center. If I leave, the others will have to work longer hours to cover my shifts and take care of my patients. Patients that happen to include Zura, who is half Pheran, loaded with medi-bot technology, and pregnant with twins."

"You know, I didn't hear you mention yourself once in that whole list. What about what you need, Alyson?" Dirk admired her devotion, but it bothered him that she always seemed to put everyone else's needs ahead of her own.

She looked at him, and it was plain from her expression, a mixture of confusion and surprise, that she didn't know the answer to his question.

"Aly, hasn't anyone ever asked you that before?" he asked.

She hesitated before answering. "I'm a doctor because I want to help others. I wouldn't be good at my job if I worried about my needs, and not theirs."

"I'm pretty sure there's a flaw in your logic, sunshine. We'll talk about that later. For now, we're going to figure out dinner and decide on room assignments."

"I can handle dinner. You might have broken my droid, but I still know how to use a food dispenser." She started to stand, but Lance stopped her with a shake of his head.

"Blade broke it, so he's on dinner duty."

She looked like she might argue, but then she sank back down onto the couch and nodded. "Okay. You guys like pizza? I've got three kinds stocked and programmed in."

"Your dispenser makes pizza? I told you guys we need to upgrade ours. Ours would have a meltdown if we tried anything that complex," Blade said, already heading to the kitchen.

"If there's anything you'd like to eat or drink, just let Huey know—once he's repaired, that is. He'll order it and program it for you. While you're not exactly guests, you're welcome to make yourselves comfortable while you're staying here. I know I haven't said it, but I'm grateful to the three of you for doing this."

"We're happy to do it," Dirk said.

"We're here for you, Doc," Blade called from the other room.

"There's nowhere else we'd rather be," Lance declared.

She burst out laughing. "If nothing else, you three are going to be great for my ego. No one is ever eager to spend time with their doctor. This might not be so bad after all."

Dirk couldn't imagine not wanting to be in Alyson's company. He just hoped that when the threat was over and she had her life back, she still wanted to spend time with them.

*

Alyson contacted Lieksa while her three new bodyguards wandered the residence in relative silence. At first, she wondered why they weren't talking, but eventually, it dawned on her that they were conversing through their private comm channel. It was like having three huge, silent predators prowling around. She hadn't had a roommate since graduating from med school, and it was strange not to be alone in her home. After a while, she went to her room to change out of her work clothes and simply have a moment of solitude.

She changed into a soft, stretchy pair of pants, a faded blue T-shirt and her favorite pair of slippers. Her friend, Phaedra, had sent them to her from some quirky little shop she'd found on some backwater space station somewhere. Phaedra's life choices meant that she never stayed in one place too long, and she loved to send Alyson knickknacks from her travels.

The slippers were lime green with purple spots. The spots lit up with every step she took, casting an ever-changing light show across the walls and floor. She loved the goofy things. No matter how hard her day, the dancing lights and eye-searing colors always improved her mood.

She was brushing out her hair when her comm device chimed. The incoming call was from Zura, and she transferred it to her wall and activated an encryption program before answering.

"Hi, Zura. How are you feeling?" she asked as her friend's face appeared on the screen.

Zura shook her head, sending her multi-hued blue hair flying. "Oh no. I didn't call to talk about me. Someone broke into your office and left you a threatening note, and you have three very hot, overprotective cyborgs staying with you as your security detail. I want to talk about that!"

"Well, that news traveled fast." Alyson sat down on the edge of her bed as she considered where to start.

"Internal comm channels make cyborgs the biggest gossips in the cosmos. Prying it out of Luke and Kit took me awhile, though. They thought it would upset me, and somehow put the twins in danger. I swear they think I turned to glass the second I got pregnant. Now, spill."

"Someone used my access code to enter my office and leave me a note. It was weird, Zura. They used red paper and folded it into a perfect pyramid. The note wasn't threatening though. It was a warning to watch my back or I wouldn't live to finish what I had started."

"*Veth*. They got through your security? Didn't you upgrade that recently?"

"Yeah, I did. And whoever it was only appeared as a faint blur on the security footage. I didn't even see it the first time I looked. Lance did, though. Once he knew that much, I didn't have a snowball's chance in a supernova of keeping them out of it."

"Of course you didn't, and you shouldn't have tried. No one else could keep you as safe as those three will. They're invested." Zura grinned. "Or they will be, once you stop fighting the inevitable. Even a blind man could see there's chemistry between all of you."

"Chemistry won't repair Huey," she muttered.

"Uh oh. Did something happen to your new droid?"

"Blade happened. They weren't in my home for thirty seconds before he tackled poor Huey and broke him. The other guys have him making dinner as penance."

Zura burst out laughing. "He tackled Huey? Oh, man. Wait until I share that with my guys. They'll never let him live it down. I hope you're making him pay for the repairs."

Alyson had already considered and dismissed the idea. "He was defending me. Well, he thought he was. I can't make him pay for trying to save my life. I've asked Lieksa to fix him up for me."

Zura's silver eyes narrowed, and she cocked her head to one side. "Seriously, how are you doing, Alyson? Is there anything me or the guys can do?"

"I'm not sure how I'm doing. I'm still processing it all. I mean, I knew there were risks. We all knew that when we signed on. Finding that note on my desk made it all too real, though. Someone out there knows what we're up to and isn't happy about it. This is a big step up from messing with my inventory shipments."

"Back up. Who is messing with your shipments? How long has this been going on?"

"Not long. A few weeks. And it's nothing major. Orders coming in short, shipments being diverted or lost in transit. It's a petty power play by the corporations. I thought it was a good sign. If they were doing that, then they couldn't know what I was really up to."

"Alyson, my friend, do I need to remind you what I do for a living?" Zura asked.

"You run a shipping business. A very successful one that keeps you far too busy to be doing favors for friends."

"Uh huh. Tell me, do those missing shipments include stuff you need to synthesize the cure?"

Alyson bit her lip. "If I say yes, you're going to roll your eyes at me, aren't you?"

Zura chuckled. "Of course I am. And then I'm going to tell you to send me a list of what you need, and I'll have it here before you know it. You should have told me sooner."

"You're not the first one to say that to me today. Apparently, I'm not good at asking for help."

"Apparently. In other unsurprising news, water is wet, and space is a tad chilly."

"Point taken. You know, when we first met I wondered how you could possibly cope with those overbearing men of yours. You were so quiet and unassuming."

Zura laughed. "In my former line of work, it worked to my advantage for everyone to underestimate me. I might have gone legit, but old habits die hard."

It was hard to imagine the diminutive half-Pheran woman as a smuggler and black marketeer, but that's what she had been raised to be. Like Alyson, she'd been expected to continue in the family business, but she had decided to forge her own path, instead. "I'll put together a list tonight and bring it over to you tomorrow."

"No, you won't. You're not leaving the med-center until the threat's eliminated," one of her new bodyguards announced from the other side of her door.

Zura winced. "They still haven't learned not to eavesdrop, huh? You can send one of the overkill triplets over tomorrow with the list…if any of them survive the night. Good luck, and watch your back."

Alyson managed to keep her temper in check until Zura signed off. "What did I tell you about listening in on private conversations?" she snapped as she headed out of her bedroom and into the hall. Dirk was standing so close to the door she barrelled into him, which only irritated her further.

"I was coming to tell you that dinner is ready and overheard you talking." He touched his ear. "Cyborg hearing, remember?"

She glared up at him. Even at five-foot-eight, she was more than a foot shorter than he was, so she had to crane her neck to meet his eyes. "I'm aware of your enhanced senses. Even if you didn't eavesdrop on purpose, you shouldn't have interjected into a private conversation. I'm certain we've had this conversation before." She knew they had because she remembered it clearly. It was the night they had met, and the first time she'd called one of them Officer Overkill. The nickname had stuck, and with good reason.

"But it isn't safe for you to go out. I thought you'd want to know that before you ended your conversation," Dirk argued.

"It was still impolite."

He frowned, but instead of continuing to argue, he lowered his head and sighed. "Will you help us with that? Our first jobs after we were freed didn't exactly require good manners. We picked up most of our social graces sitting around freighter galleys and mining ship mess halls. If you told us what we're doing wrong, maybe we'd be less irritating." He grinned, and her heart beat a little faster just watching him. "Or maybe not. We've been told we're a handful."

The request caught her off guard, and by the time she answered him, her anger was gone. "I'd be happy to do that."

"Good." Dirk reached up to tuck a strand of her hair behind her ear, stroking his fingers across her cheek. "I don't like it when you're angry with me."

"I wasn't angry." And when he touched her like that, she couldn't imagine ever being mad at him again.

He chuckled and raised a dark brow, a move that made him look even sexier. "Oh yeah, you were. And I imagine you're going to be mad at us again before this is over. Try to remember, anything we do, we're doing to keep you safe."

"I'll try. But I've been making my own choices and living by my rules for a long time now. When I make you crazy, try to remember that, too. Okay?"

Dirk leaned down, nuzzled her hair, and whispered in her ear. "Aly, you've been making me crazy since the day we met. I don't expect that's ever going to change, and I don't want it to."

The floor tilted and spun away and her breath caught in her throat. Before she could think of anything to say, he moved away again, and Blade called from the kitchen. "Dinner's ready. Get in here before Lance and I eat all of this delicious bounty."

"He's not kidding. That's probably something we should work into our lessons on good manners," Dirk said.

"I'll put it near the top of the list."

"Right after a refresher course on eavesdropping?"

"Exactly."

* * * *

Dinner was a boisterous, laughter-filled affair. The brothers took turns telling her about the jobs they had held and the places they'd worked in the years since they were freed. Most of the stories involved embarrassing moments that had the victim groaning denials and insisting the others were lying.

The guys shooed her out of the kitchen after dinner without letting her clear away so much as a fork. She left them to clean and went to her office to check incoming messages and compile the list of items Zura had requested. It felt strange to leave the work to someone else. She'd spent most of her life doing things for herself. Her maternal grandparents were the only ones she trusted to be there for her. Everyone else had always been too busy with their own lives and plans.

In an attempt to appease her bodyguards, she left the office door open. Every ten minutes or so one of them would pass by, but they didn't disturb her. Their consideration gave her hope that they could make this work. After an hour, Blade dropped in to let her know he was heading back to their residence cubby to pick up what they'd need for their stay. He even remembered to knock and didn't stay any longer than it took for him to convey his message.

She kept working until her back ached and her eyes felt gritty. When she'd decided to become a doctor, no one had warned her that for every hour she spent with patients, she would spend two more filling out reports and keeping up with the day to day business of running a med-center. When she yawned for the third time, she decided it was time for a cup of tea. That would keep her going for another hour or so. She headed to the kitchen, and stopped short when Dirk appeared in the hall in front of her.

"Your bedroom is in the other direction."

"Yes, it is. But the kitchen is where the tea is." She tried to step around him, but he folded his arms across his chest and moved in front of her again.

"You don't need tea. You need sleep."

"I'm fine. I learned to go without sleep while I was in med school." She tapped his forearm with her finger. "So, if you'd get out of my way I'll go get my tea."

"Not going to happen. You've had a hell of a day, and you're exhausted. I'm not a doctor, but even I can tell you're pushing yourself too hard."

She stifled another yawn and pointed toward the kitchen. "I'll sleep in an hour. I promise."

"Are you always this stubborn?" he asked, but his lips were turned up into a grin that belied the annoyed tone in his voice.

"Always." She hadn't gotten this far in her career, or her life, by backing down, and she wasn't going to start now.

"Noted. But you're still not getting your way. Not this time."

He moved so fast she didn't have time to do more than blink before he bent over and hauled her over one massive shoulder. When he straightened, she yelped in surprise and started kicking and squirming. She knew it was hopeless, but she wasn't going to suffer through this indignity without a fight. Her fuzzy slippers thumped against his side, and every time they connected, dots of purple lights danced across the walls and ceiling.

Put me down, you jerk!"

He clamped an arm across the back of her thighs, locking down her legs and started walking down the hall, away from the kitchen. "I'll put you down when we get to your bedroom."

She smacked her hand against his ass, which was the only part of him she could reach as she dangled off his shoulder. "I was wrong. You're not a jerk. You're an asshole. You know what's worse than eavesdropping? This. This is worse."

A door slid open somewhere in front of them, but all she could see was Dirk's broad back.

"I heard yelling. Is everything okay?"

She wriggled again. "No, it's not. You're supposed to be my bodyguard, so help me! Make Dirk put me down right now."

"Uh, Dirk, is there a reason our protectee is upside down and royally pissed off?"

"She needs to go to bed and is too stubborn to admit it. So, I'm escorting her there."

"Uh huh." Blade appeared beside her, grinning from ear-to-ear. "Cute slippers."

"You're not going to help?"

"I'm not. You need rest. You aren't any good to anyone if you're too tired to think."

"You're both assholes." She gave up arguing and went limp.

"Yeah, but we're still right. Good night, Doc." Blade gave her a jaunty wave and vanished from sight again, still chuckling.

Dirk carried her to her room, which gave her a few uninterrupted seconds to get intimately acquainted with his body. At least his hard muscles and the tight curve of his ass were a distraction from her embarrassment at being carried around like an old-fashioned sack of grain.

Instead of setting her back on her feet, he lowered her carefully onto her bed, nestling her into the blankets with surprising tenderness.

"Goodnight, Alyson. Sleep well."

She frowned up at him. "I'm tempted to lie awake all night just to spite you."

He chuckled as he stood up. "I don't doubt it. But you're too smart to do that. I'll see you in the morning."

She stuck her tongue out for a second but stopped when it struck her that she was being childish. Asshole or not, Dirk and his brothers had put their lives on hold to protect her. "Sleep well."

"Thank you, but I'm not planning on sleeping. I lost tonight's round of rock, paper, scissors, so I'm on watch."

She sat up and stared at him. "You're going to stay up all night?"

"Uh huh. If you need me, I'll be on the other side of your door. No one is getting to you without coming through me, first."

"You need your sleep, too."

"I'm a cyborg with a body loaded with medi-bots. I don't need to sleep. At least, not for a few days."

"Do you need a blanket? Something to read?" It bothered her to think of him sitting in the empty hall all night, alone and far from comfortable.

"Go to sleep, Aly. I'll be fine."

He left her room, and she lay quietly, listening to him settle in the hall outside her door. She got up, changed into a pair of pajamas and prepared for bed. Before she got back under the covers, she crossed to the door and pressed her hand against it. "Good night, Dirk. Thank you for watching over me."

"Get back in bed before I come in there and tuck you in myself."

She refused to admit how tempting his offer was. Not even to herself. She went to bed and drifted off to sleep, part of her still acutely aware of the man on guard outside. It was comforting to know he was there. Despite the disruptions and chaos they caused, this was going to work out for them, she was certain of it.

CHAPTER FIVE

"Why did I ever think this was a good idea?" Alyson pushed past Blade to get to her desk.

He could've moved back another inch or two, but that would have meant missing out on a chance to breathe in her perfume and feel her brush against him on her way by. He wanted more than that, but after two days of non-stop togetherness, the lovely doctor was still resisting the pull between them. It was making him crazy.

"Because it is a good idea. You need protecting, and we're the best ones for the job." As far as Blade was concerned, they were the only ones to do it. If she tried to replace them, they'd give a vivid demonstration of their skills while taking down any possible rival. She was theirs to protect. End of discussion.

"You've all said that, but I'm still not sure why you think so."

He straightened to his full height and pointed to the Corp-Sec badge affixed to the chest of his deep red tunic. "We're Corporate Security, for one thing. We didn't get this gig because we look good in the uniform."

"I hate to point this out, but the guy who tried to kill your bosses was Corp-Sec, too. What else have you got?"

He leaned back against the wall and shrugged. "It's what we were designed for."

Alyson's head snapped up. "You were?"

It wasn't something he talked about. Like most of his kind, Blade didn't dwell on his unusual creation or the fact that his skills and abilities had been hardwired into his brain instead of learned over time. "We were created to protect high priority targets. High ranking officials, corporate royalty, and VIPs. I've got a head full of tactics and strategies all pertaining to keeping you alive at all costs. So, when we tell you there's no one better, we mean it. Astek designed us to protect their most valuable assets, and they made sure we had every enhancement you can think of so we could do the job right."

"So when you say you're the best…"

"We meant it. I know this hasn't been easy for you, Doc, but we know what we're doing."

She snorted with laughter. "Is that why my poor droid needed emergency surgery? Lieksa couldn't believe how much damage you did with one tackle."

"Like I said, we know what we're doing. I still feel bad about Huey. Even if it gave Lance a chance to play repair tech. He loves tinkering with stuff like that."

"I noticed. I thought that might be part of what you were programmed for, but it can't be." She set down her stylus and leaned forward in her chair. "So, Lance likes fixing things. What about you? What do you do for fun?"

Blade almost gave her his standard, flippant answer, the one involving bars, booze, and bad decisions, but he didn't. Instead, he offered her the truth and hoped she didn't laugh at him.

"Games, mostly. Not vid games. Those are fun, but I'm talking about games that require logic and strategy."

"You mean like chess?"

There was no judgment in her tone, so he kept going. "Yeah, exactly. Did you know there are hundreds of versions of chess? And that's not including the Pheran and Torski variants."

This was usually when people's eyes glazed over, but Alyson smiled broadly and nodded with obvious enthusiasm. He felt like he had won the damned lottery.

"Have you ever played Fortress chess? That's one of my favorites, but it requires four players. I haven't played since I left home," she asked.

Re'veth. He had won the lottery.

"I've heard of it. Never tried it, though." A thought occurred to him, and he took a chance. "You know, there are four of us living upstairs at the moment. You could teach us how to play. Maybe tonight?"

When she nodded, his heart did a triple beat of joy that was as close as he could get to a victory dance. Not only had he found something for the four of them to do together, but he'd discovered that he and the sexy doctor shared more than sizzling hot chemistry. They liked the same game. It wasn't much, but it was a start.

They spent a few idyllic moments talking strategy and their preferred variation of the game, but it wasn't long before they were interrupted by her comm device. The *fraxxing* thing seemed to go off constantly. It amazed him how much she got done considering the number of times a day she was interrupted.

She read the incoming message and uttered a low groan. "We've got a *crimson* overdose victim coming in. He's highly agitated and aggressive enough they've already got him in restraints."

"That sounds dangerous. Can't someone else deal with him?"

She got to her feet. "No. I have the most experience with these cases. I have to attend. I know you guys only want me treating familiar patients, but this is different. There's a life at stake."

"Yeah, yours."

"And if this patient dies, then I'll have to live with that for the rest of my life. Not happening. My life isn't more valuable than his."

"You're a doctor, and he's an idiot who took *crimson*. Newsflash for you, doc. Your life *is* worth more than his."

She shot him a look cold enough to frost a dozen ales. "I'm still going. If it eases your mind, you can come, too."

"Damn right I'm going with you." He followed her out of the office and across the med-center to an area he hadn't been in before. Judging by the eerie quiet, they were the only ones around.

"In here." She moved through a pair of swinging doors before he could get ahead of her.

"Next time, wait until I've cleared the room." Until now, she hadn't allowed them into the treatment rooms when patients were present, but she had agreed to let them check the area before the patient was brought in.

"Please. Lance is standing guard out front, and I don't think he'd let a dust mote get past him without the proper ID. We've got about three minutes before all hell breaks loose, so here's what's going to happen. You're going to stand over there, out of the way. If I need you, I'll tell you."

"Anyone tell you you're hot as hell when you're barking orders?"

"No one who lived." She shot back without even looking at him. She was busy organizing trays of equipment, and her focus was on that, not him.

"Sassy is sexy. You keep this up, I might wind up proposing." She had no idea how much truth was in that statement. They weren't there yet, but if the stars aligned, then one day, he believed the four of them would get there. She was like no other woman they'd ever met. His head insisted it was too early to be certain, but his heart was already convinced she was the one.

"Flirt later. Right now, I need your help." She pushed a cart in his direction. "That goes beside the bed."

By the time he had the cart in place, the room was starting to fill with people. Since all of them knew the procedures better than he did, he moved to the spot Alyson had pointed to and tried to stay out of the way. It was like watching a dance performance, only instead of music, the movements were accompanied by queries and commands in a language he couldn't understand. It had a cadence and rhythm all its own, though, all of it leading up to a crescendo when the doors flew open and the medics arrived with their patient.

It was the first time Blade had seen the effects of a *crimson* overdose up close, and it made him question the sanity of anyone who took the drug. The victim was a human male, though he was bellowing loud enough to sound like an enraged Torski. What little hair he had was plastered to his scalp, and his lips and chin were flecked with bloody foam. Rivulets of blood flowed down his face from a head wound, soaking the thin pillow under his head.

"Don't touch me! *Fraxxing* bastards. I'll kill you. All of ya. Get away. Leave me alone." His enraged screams rose to a deafening volume as the medical team closed in and got to work.

Alyson seemed to be everywhere at once, issuing orders in a brisk, composed tone that kept everyone focused and moving. He stood in awe as she and her team somehow managed to treat the combative and abusive victim, but despite their efforts, he could see they were losing the fight.

Crimson, taken in small doses, was a non-addictive hallucinogenic pharma that left the user feeling euphoric and mellow. But take too much, or too many doses over a lifetime, and the euphoria gave way to uncontrolled rage and violence that often left the victim comatose or dead. Judging by the man's uneven breaths and delirium, he wasn't going to last much longer. The drug would tear his body apart if Alyson and her team couldn't stop the progression soon.

She was bent over her patient, trying to inject something into his neck when it happened. There was a horrific sound: a sickening tearing, popping noise that made Blade's stomach lurch. Then the patient suddenly tried to sit up, smashing his head into Alyson's and sending her staggering backward.

Blade launched himself across the room, knocking aside people and equipment to reach Alyson. She was still on her feet when he got to her, but it was touch and go. She swayed back and forth, too stunned by the blow to do anything.

"I've got you." He wrapped an arm around her shoulders and pulled her close before leading her away from the table. It wasn't until he was satisfied she was out of harm's way that he took a good look at the scene and realized what had happened. The overdose victim had torn an arm out of the restraints, but in freeing himself, he had done terrible damage to his body. His arm was broken at the elbow, the flesh torn apart as torrents of blood flowed over the damaged and dangling limb.

The rest of the medical team managed to get their patient restrained again, though the constant bellows and cursing continued.

"I have to help." She started to pull away, but Blade locked his arm around her waist.

"You can't help him. You need to sit down. If there was a spare doctor around this place, I'd be taking you to see them right now, but everyone's a little busy with that guy."

"I need to do my job…just as soon as the room stops spinning."

Right. That's it. We're out of here." He tapped the nearest staff member on the shoulder. "I'm taking Dr. Jefferies outside."

The older man glanced over at him and nodded in approval. "Good. Alyson, you know we're going to lose this one no matter what. You don't need to be here to watch."

"I like him already." He half carried Alyson out of the room, ignoring her protests and half-hearted attempts to break out of his hold.

"You're only saying that because Dr. Basque agreed with you. If I were in there, maybe I could do something."

"Your team knows what they're doing. *Veth*, woman. I'm no doctor, and even I could see you were going to lose him. You can't save them all."

She uttered a pained sigh. "I have to try, though."

"I know. And I admire that about you. But not when you're putting yourself in danger to do it. Come on, we're going back to your office to have that bump on your head looked at."

"By who? Like you said, all my staff are back in there."

"One second, I'm calling in the reinforcements." He kept walking as he contacted Dirk via their private comm channel.

"Dirk, get your ass to Alyson's office. Bring a med-kit."

"The med-kit better be for you, or I'm going to kick your butt from here to the Hercules Cluster."

"It's for Alyson. A patient broke out of their restraints and head butted her. She's fine. In fact, she's arguing with me and trying to get back to her patient right now."

"She'd do that even if she was bleeding out and missing a limb. I'll see you downstairs shortly...and for the record, you suck at being a bodyguard."

Blade couldn't argue with Dirk's assessment. Alyson had gotten hurt on his watch. That couldn't happen again. It shouldn't have happened at all. He had to do better.

* * * *

Alyson sensed Blade's withdrawal. He was a Corp-Sec officer, so it couldn't be the violence or the bloody scene they had left behind, but something had him subdued and quiet. They were almost to her office before he spoke again.

"Dirk's on his way. He's going to check that bump on your head, and then I suspect he's going tear into me for letting you get hurt."

Understanding dawned. He blamed himself for what had happened, which was ridiculous.

"You didn't *let* me get hurt. I shouldn't have gotten that close. It was my mistake."

She keyed in her access code, but her hands were trembling and she had to do it again before it worked. The adrenaline rush that came with every emergency was fading, now she was out of the room. That, combined with the blow to her head, had affected her more than she had realized. Or maybe it was the fact Blade still had his arm around her, his hard body tucked behind hers.

"I don't see it that way, and neither will my brothers." He took her hand in his and squeezed it. "You're shaking. Stay here while I check the room, and then I want you off your feet. Are you sure you're alright?"

"I'm fine. I've got a bump on the head and a four-alarm headache, that's all. And why is Dirk coming down here? I'm a damned doctor, I'd know if there was a problem."

"Sit. If you try to leave that chair before Dirk gets here, he'll blame me. Then we'll get into a fight, I'll have to kick his ass, and you'll have two more patients to deal with."

"You two would have to do some serious damage to each other before you needed my help. Your medi-bots make sure you heal amazingly fast."

"Do you have any siblings? Brothers, specifically?" He asked.

"I have a brother, but he was older than me by enough years that we didn't spend much time together. I have plenty of cousins though. Why?"

"Did your cousins fight a lot? I bet they did. So, you know what it's like when brothers fight. Now, add in the fact we were designed to be the perfect soldiers, and finish it off with the fact that you're important to all three of us…it's going to get personal."

"You'd beat the hell out of each other over me?"

Blade crouched at her side, so they were eye to eye. "Don't you get it, yet? When it comes to you, there's nothing we wouldn't do."

"But—"

"No buts. No arguments. That's the way it is, Doc. There's nothing you can say that's going to change it." He leaned until their mouths were nearly touching. "You're ours to protect. One day, soon I hope, you're going to be ours, period. That's what we want."

"What if I don't want that?" She asked, but she knew it wasn't true. It had never been true, and that terrified her.

"Then we'll keep doing what we've been doing."

"What's that?"

His green eyes lit up with desire as he moved in closer still. "Proving that you want us as much as we want you." He closed the last bit of space between them and kissed her.

She should have pulled away or turned her head, but her heart didn't let her. Not this time. Instead, she buried her hands in his dark hair and held on as if her life depended on it. His lips slanted across hers, and the groan that rose from his throat was one of pure need. He cupped her cheek in one hand, stroking her skin with his thumb as he took the kiss deeper, pressing her back into the chair.

He stroked a hand up her thigh, working slowly higher, and the heat of his touch was enough to melt the last shreds of doubt. This was what she wanted. No, it was what she'd been craving since the day the brothers had crash landed into her life.

"Really? You kissed *him* first. He let you get hurt, and now you're rewarding him."

She hadn't realized they weren't alone anymore, but Dirk was standing in the doorway with a look of wry exasperation on his face.

"If I claim the head injury was messing with my judgment, you're going to freak out and decide I have a concussion, aren't you?"

"There's nothing wrong with your judgment. Or any other part of you." Blade stroked her cheek again before standing up and turning to face his brother. "She's fine, but I know you'd want to check for yourself."

Dirk walked to her desk and set down a med-kit. "How are you feeling? Headache? Any nausea or dizziness?"

"A patient suffering from a *crimson* overdose broke his own arm and tore his shoulder out of its socket, then head-butted me. Yes, I have a headache. I need a pain-blocker and some coffee. That's all."

"I'll be the judge of that."

"And what qualifies you to judge anything of the sort? Last I checked, I was the only one in this room with a license to practice medicine."

"I've worked as a medic on a couple of our contracts," Dirk said.

"You're a medic?"

"More or less."

"So why are you in Corp-Sec and not working here?"

Silence. Followed by Blade snickering quietly before commenting. "You've rendered him speechless. I didn't know that was possible."

"It never occurred to me you'd want me here. I'm not certified. All three of us have extensive medical knowledge hardwired into our heads in case we needed it to save an asset's life. The rest I picked up along the way."

"You can get certified. I'm helping Lieksa do that right now."

Dirk shook his head. "I tried that. I couldn't find anyone interested in certifying a cyborg. We might be free, but we haven't been welcomed with open arms. We're too different. Too dangerous."

She snorted. "You're only dangerous to idiots, criminals, and household droids. If you ever decide you want to change careers, I can get you certified."

"We'll talk about my career plans another time. Right now, I'd like to take a look at the bump on your head. May I?" Dirk opened the kit and pulled out a bio-scanner.

"If I say no, are you going to toss me over your shoulder and make me do it anyway?"

"As tempting as that sounds, I wouldn't. The last thing you need is to be upside down. That isn't going to help your headache."

"In that case, go ahead. I know you're not going to find anything, but you're almost as stubborn as I am." The truth was, they were probably all more stubborn than she was, but there was no way she would ever admit it. They were cocky enough as it was.

It didn't take long for Dirk to examine her. He was efficient, asking the right questions and handling the scanner with easy familiarity before finally admitting that her assessment was right. She was fine.

"I told you so. Having watched you work, I think you'd make a great medic," she said as he put away the scanner and selected a basic pain-blocker from the kit.

He handed her the meds, still in their container so she could see what he was giving her. "Thanks. You really think you could get me certified? I like Corp-Sec, but it's nice to know there might be another option."

She took the medication and washed it down with a swig of cold coffee. "Out here on the Drift, the rules are different. You know that. Anywhere else in the galaxy, I'd be considered too young and inexperienced to run my own med-center."

"Anyone who watches you work would never think of you as inexperienced. You were incredible today," Blade said.

"I wasn't good enough, though. He was too far gone for me to save."

"And yet, you're still regretting that you didn't go back and try anyway. He made his choice when he took *crimson*. Everyone knows how dangerous it is, Doc."

"I walked out on a patient."

Dirk made a noise of strangled frustration. "If any of your staff had been the one to get hurt, would you have let them stay?"

"Of course not. They're my responsibility. I would never…" She trailed off and narrowed her eyes at him. "I see what you're trying to do, but it's not the same thing."

"They're your responsibility, and you're ours. Blade got you out of there because it was the right choice." Dirk shot a dark look at his brother. "Especially considering he let you get hurt in the first place."

"He didn't! He was letting me do my job."

"And you need to let us do ours," Dirk said.

"I'll try. Okay? Now, will you let me talk to my staff and find out what happened after I left? I can make sure they're alright, and then I'll come right back here."

"You can check in with your staff, but after that, you're going to call it a day. Deal?" Dirk said.

Alyson considered arguing, but she simply didn't have the energy. Her head was throbbing, and she was too distracted by everything that had happened to do any real work. "Deal. But only if Blade does me a favor."

"Anything you like, Doc. All you have to do is ask."

"See if you can find a Fortress chessboard for tonight."

"With pleasure." Blade returned to her side, crouched down, and brushed a quick kiss across her cheek. "I'll see you upstairs. Try not to get any more bumps or bruises today, okay?"

She turned her head to kiss him properly. "I'll do my best."

Dirk groaned. "And there you go, kissing him again. And what's this about chess? You're clearly spending too much time with Blade. I'm changing the duty roster tomorrow. You're going to be spending the day with me."

"I want to keep spending time with all of you." She hesitated before adding. "I never want to have to choose who to spend time with, and who to exclude."

Both men exhaled sharply, but Dirk spoke first. "If this goes the way we hope it will, none of us will ever be excluded."

"That's what I'm hoping for, too." Her head still wasn't sure this was the right call, but logic wasn't in the driver's seat any longer. From the moment she had kissed Blade, her heart had taken control. Now, all she could do is buckle in, hang on, and hope her heart knew how to navigate the asteroid field of potential heartache she had just flown into.

CHAPTER SIX

After treating Alyson's injury yesterday, Dirk had a question he needed to ask her, but he didn't want to do it with his brothers around. He had a better chance of talking about it with her if she didn't feel like they were all teaming up on her.

Officially, she had the day off, but that only meant she was working in her upstairs office instead of in the med-center. Alyson worked harder than anyone he'd ever met, and it worried him. She couldn't keep up this pace much longer, and for some reason, she hadn't gone with the obvious solution – injecting herself with the medibots.

He knocked on her office door. "You have a minute?"

"Come on in. I'm expecting a call from my friend, Phaedra, but she lives in her own personal time zone, so I have no idea when she'll actually get in contact."

He had to duck to get through the doorway. Alyson's home was spacious, but the doors were still designed with normal humans in mind. The office itself was a decent size, but it felt small and cozy because of the clutter of personal items and photos that filled the shelves. There was a hand-knitted shawl hanging off the back of her chair, and the desk looked like it was made of real wood and not imitation. He took a seat and nodded. "Hi."

"Hi." She tipped her head to the side and asked, "What brings you by? If you're worried about the bump on my head, it's gone. And while I'm saddened we lost the overdose victim, I'm not in here beating myself up over what happened."

"I'm glad you're feeling better, but that's not why I'm here. I've been wondering why you haven't used some of Zale's medi-bots. He's offered it to everyone now, and it's obvious you don't have them. Why not?"

"You answered your own question. I'm being watched. Right now, all they see is a tired doctor working long hours. What do you think would happen if I suddenly looked refreshed and energetic no matter how hard I was working?"

"They'd suspect something."

"The corporations have already made it clear that they don't like me treating cyborgs, and they will bury me in lawsuits and even criminal charges if I try to research or recreate any aspect of you and your brethren's cybernetic components. If they thought I was using it on myself, I'd already be in custody. They don't know about the medi-bots. Whoever is targeting me wants to stop me before I find a way to reverse what they did to the female cyborgs." She sat up a little straighter in her chair, and her hands closed into fists. "I will, too. Soon. At least, I will so long as you and your brothers can keep me safe."

"You know we will. If you had our accelerated healing, though, I would worry a little less. You're vulnerable, Alyson. I wish you'd reconsider. You're sacrificing your health, and possibly your life, to keep this secret."

"I have to. At least for a little while longer. The last thing the corporations want is for their medibot technology to spread into the non-cyborg population. They'll do anything to prevent that. They have to suspect that Zura is carrying medibots now, but they can't prove it since I refused to give them any of her medical files or the data I collected on her. I have to finish the cure and get it disseminated before anyone outside our group learns that Zura is pregnant. Once they know, they'll come for her."

She reached into her top drawer and drew out an injector that he assumed was loaded with a dose of the nanotech that Zale had given all the non-cyborgs members of their group. "Until then, this stays here. When it's safe to use it, I will."

Dirk didn't like it, but he had to admit that Alyson had a point. It just didn't sit well with him that she was paying such a high price to protect everyone else.

"You're an amazing woman. Too stubborn for your own good, but still amazing. I promise that

Lance, Blade, and I will make sure you finish everything you want to accomplish. And the second it's done, I want you to take the damned injection and make sure you live to see the all changes you're going to make."

"You say that like you won't be around to make sure I do it."

He could have lied to her, but he didn't. She needed to know that they were willing to make sacrifices, too. "I might not. The work you're doing is too important, and you're the only one who can do it. I'm expendable, you're not."

"No one is expendable. No. One." She rose from her chair and rounded her desk to stand in front of him. She had her hands on her hips, and her gray eyes were as hard as flint as she stared him down.

"I am. It's what I was designed to be. They might have deactivated the behavioral programming, but the drive to protect is still there. It's always been part of me." He rose to his feet and gathered her into his arms. "It's just that until now, I've never had someone in my life I was willing to die for."

"I don't—"

He stopped her words with a kiss. If it came to it, he wouldn't regret dying for her. Not if he could spend the time he had left like this.

She tasted sweeter than he had imagined, like sun-ripened strawberries. He'd only tasted such bounty once, and he never imagined he would taste it again. He tightened his arms around her, needing to feel her body pressed against his. She moaned into his mouth as she rose up on her toes to meet his kiss and return it with one of her own. He felt like he'd been doused in rocket fuel and tossed into the nearest star. Heat sizzled across his skin, fueled by the flames of need burning inside him.

Unable to resist, he took it farther, sliding a hand down to her ass and pulling her in tight against the hard shaft of his cock. She gasped, opening her mouth enough for him to sweep his tongue inside. Her tongue tangled with his as she fisted his shirt in her hands, and he knew she was feeling the same wild need that drove him. They had been destined for this moment from the first time they'd met.

"That was worth the wait," he muttered, unaware he was speaking aloud until Alyson laughed.

"Is that your way of saying I should have given in weeks ago?"

"I admit to nothing." He lifted his head to smile at her. "Though, it's possible I'm pissed with myself for moving so slow that Blade got to kiss you before I did."

"Please, tell me the three of you aren't keeping score. Or worse, you've got bets on how this is going to unfold."

"We're not betting on anything. Now, I've heard rumors that the rest of the group have a pool going, but you'll have to take it up with them."

"They don't!" She closed her eyes and groaned. "Who am I kidding. Of course they do. I bet Zura's brother Royan is the ringleader, too."

"If it bothers you, I'll put a stop to it."

She shook her head. "It's a little embarrassing, but I'll live. I didn't realize everyone was aware that we were…uh, headed this way."

"As you've pointed out more than once, we're not subtle men. Given how close this group is, it isn't surprising that they figured it out. You have a lot of friends watching out for you, Aly."

"They're your friends, too. You're just as much a part of this weird, slightly insane family as I am." She paused, then added. "They're an amazing group, aren't they? I've never known anyone who watches out for each other the way they do. Like a proper family."

She was right. He and his brothers had all been accepted into the group. After years of being outsiders, of never quite fitting in, the easy acceptance and friendship this group offered them was something they were still adjusting to. "Yeah, I know. We even got the threatening speech from your adoptive big brothers about what they'd do to us if we broke your heart. It was…disturbingly graphic."

"They threatened you? I'll kill them. No, I can't do that, it's against my oath. I've got a better plan.

I'll tell their wives and girlfriends what they did." Her eyes gleamed with mischief. "Tell me who it was, and I'll take care of it."

"And then they'll toss me out an airlock for ratting them out. Not a chance. Besides, they were looking out for you. I can't blame them for that. They're going to need some time to get used to the fact that watching out for you is my job now, not theirs."

"You know, I'm actually pretty good at taking care of myself. I've been doing it for a long time now," Alyson retorted.

Dirk was about to argue, but he was interrupted by a series of strident chirps and whistles that made them both wince.

"What in starsfury is that noise?" he asked.

"That would be Phaedra. She likes to make an entrance, even when she's not actually here."

*

Alyson untangled herself from Dirk and scrambled to retrieve the comm unit lying on her desk. She activated the vid screen and smiled as her friend's face appeared. Her smile faded the second she saw Phaedra's expression. Something had her normally fearless friend rattled.

"What the *fraxxing* hell have you got me into, Alyson? I found the info you wanted, and it's hotter than a supernova."

Dirk cursed under his breath, then asked, "More trouble?"

Phaedra stared past Alyson. "Who is that and why is he listening in?"

"That's Dirk. He's one of my bodyguards."

"You have bodyguards now?" Phae tossed the weight of her fuchsia curls back from her face and locked eyes with Alyson. "Why do you need bodyguards?"

"Someone broke into my office and left me a note warning me to watch my back or I wouldn't live much longer. Dirk and his brothers are protecting me."

Phae grinned for a second. "Do the other two brothers look like him? Can I borrow them when I get there?"

"We're identical triplets, and no, you can't borrow us. We're Alyson's."

She pouted. "I'm going to need someone to watch my ass when I get to the Drift. You're in charge of finding me some hot bodyguards of my own."

"Why are you coming here, and what did you find? Are you okay? Why do you need bodyguards?" If she'd put Phaedra in danger, she was never going to forgive herself. Phaedra found enough trouble on her own, she didn't need help from her friends.

"I'm fine, for now. Someone managed to back trace my last data dive, and I had to take off in a hurry. A bunch of guys in black outfits with some big damned guns showed up at my door less than an hour after I retrieved your data. It was buried behind some serious military-grade security."

"Can you tell me anything about it? This might be incredibly important, Phae."

She snorted with laughter. "Yeah, I figured that much out when the men in black started kicking down my door. Fortunately, I was already gone by then. Those DNA samples you sent me all have one thing in common. They're from IAF soldiers. Part of something called the Vault of the Fallen."

"You hacked the Interstellar Armed Forces? Phae, I didn't ask you to do that."

Her friend grinned. "I know. That was all me, and it was fun. The running for my life part, that's been a little less enjoyable. The thing is, I don't think it's the IAF that came after me. The ones that showed up at my place weren't wearing uniforms."

"How do you know that?" Dirk asked.

"I live a wild and interesting life, big guy. Because of that, I'm a believer in extensive security measures. Like perimeter alarms and motion activated vid monitors that sent me everything they recorded right up to when the bad men with guns broke my toys."

"You're safe though, right? And you're really coming here?" Alyson hadn't seen Phaedra in years.

"Whatever you've gotten yourself into, it's dangerous. You've never once asked for my help before. You need your friends, so I'm coming to you."

Alyson reached out to touch the screen of her comm device, still stunned by the fact that Phaedra was on her way here. "Thanks, Phae."

Phaedra snorted. "Like I'd be anywhere else right now. My friend needs me, so I'm on my way. I'll be there in a week. Cargo freighter isn't the most comfortable way to travel, or the fastest, but if you pay them enough, it's easy to be anonymous." She held up a data stick. "Everything you need to know is on here. I'll send you the encryption key first, then the data. When I get there, you're going to tell me what the hell this is all about. Until then, I don't want to know. It's safer that way."

"You didn't answer my question, Phae. Are you safe?"

"Safe enough." Phaedra glanced over at Dirk. "You better keep my friend safe and sound until I get there, big guy. If anything happens to her, I'll make you sorry you were ever born."

Dirk chuckled. "That would be hard to do, considering I wasn't born at all." He raised his hands and pointed to the barcode on his left wrist. "Don't worry about Aly. We're not going to let anything happen to her. She's important to us."

Phaedra's brows rose. "Aly, huh? Sounds like they're not just your bodyguards. Praise the stars above, are you finally getting some? And cyborgs! I've heard some stories about them, you lucky girl. I expect to hear every detail once I'm there. And don't bother telling me to mind my own business, we both know that isn't going to happen."

Phaedra took secrets as a challenge. She plugged herself into the cyberworld, and dug up every nugget of information she could. "Details when you get here, I promise, but I'm not—I mean, we're not—forget it. I'll explain later. Behave yourself until then, would you?"

"Me? Never. They're bringing the FLT drive online in a few minutes. Time for me to buckle up." Phaedra blew a kiss off the tips of her fingers. "See you in four days."

She was gone before Alyson could do more than wave goodbye.

"Your best friend is uh, interesting. Do you realize she never actually told you when she was getting here? She said a week, then four days."

"You don't need to be diplomatic. I know Phae's a lunatic with no filter and a genius IQ. She's also incredibly paranoid. However she's getting here, it's not by freighter. No freighter could get here in three days. And that's when she'll be arriving. Seven days in a week, subtract four days, and that's when she's due to arrive. Like I said, paranoid and brilliant. I'm just grateful she usually uses her talents for good. Otherwise, she'd probably be ruling the galaxy by now."

"She hacked the IAF."

"For me, and for our cause. That means it was for the greater good. Do you know anyone else who could have gotten us that information? If it's true, then you and all the other cyborgs were created with the help of the IAF. That's worrisome, considering the military have always claimed they weren't involved in any part of the Resource Wars or the creation of cyborg soldiers."

"I know." Dirk scrubbed a hand over his face. "This means the list of people who want you stopped just got a lot longer. We need to take a look at the data she's going to send over, then call the others and figure out what comes next."

"Are you sorry you signed on with us, yet?" She wouldn't blame him if he did. This was turning out to be more dangerous than any of them had expected. A smart man would walk away now, while he still could.

"Why would I be sorry? This is important. *Fraxx*, it might be the most important thing I do in my whole life." He moved in and drew her into his arms again. "Protecting you and getting a chance to be in your life, that's worth any risk."

"You know you don't have to risk it all to be in my life, don't you?" She worried about what might happen. Not only to her, but to all of them. Especially to the three men determined to protect her at any cost. They might be ready to sacrifice themselves for her, but she wasn't ready to let them do it. They were too important to her.

* * * *

Lance wanted to pace, but there were too many people crowded into Alyson's living room for him to do that. They were all there, listening intently as

Alyson explained to their gathered friends what was in the data file she had been sent. By the time she was finished speaking, it was clear to all of them that they had stepped into the path of a comet none of them had seen coming. Every single cyborg DNA sample Alyson had collected could be traced to the IAF's Vault of the Fallen, whatever that was. It sounded ominous and more than a little creepy. All Phaedra had managed to find out before she went on the run was that it was a repository of some kind, a genetic vault containing the DNA of the best and brightest soldiers to ever grace their ranks. Those men and women were the ancestors of the cyborgs.

"You're telling me that when Kit and Luke injected me with their medi-bots, the transfer worked because somewhere in my family tree is a soldier whose DNA is part of this Fallen project?" Zura asked, her silver eyes wide with shock.

"It appears so. Do you know who that might be?" Alyson asked.

"The only person I can think of is my great-grandfather, Tanner Watson. He was an IAF pilot. He was a bit of a legend, at least to hear Dad talk about him. I never knew whether to believe him or not."

Kit chuckled and looked down at his wife. "Another pilot in the family. What a shock."

"Yep. It's in our blood. My future nephews are going to be awesome pilots, just like their uncle,"

Royan declared, then caught his sister's frown and added, "I mean, like their uncle, and their mom."

"You just volunteered yourself for the next run to the Traffa system, little brother."

"*Fraxx*. C'mon, Zura. I just got back from my last run six hours ago."

"Which means you have all night to rest up before you take the *Sun Sprite* out again. And before anyone asks, I have no idea if the twins are boys are girls. We've decided we want to be surprised."

Lieksa laughed. "I bet Alyson knows, though. Don't you, Doc?"

Alyson smiled for the first time since speaking with Phaedra. "No comment."

"Which means you do know. When the baby pool starts, you're not allowed to bet on gender," Royan said.

Dirk groaned. "You've done it now. You had to bring up betting pools."

Alyson scowled at Royan. "I heard you were betting on my love life, you scoundrel." She held out a hand. "I'll be taking half your profits on that little enterprise. Just don't tell me what the odds are, or who bet on what. I don't want to know."

Everyone laughed, and some of the tension that had gripped the room during Alyson's update receded.

After that, the conversation ebbed and flowed as they discussed what they had learned, and what it might mean. The IAF was in charge of defending all of humanity, their territories, and the governments that ruled them. Their role included keeping the corporations in check. If the IAF was compromised, then it was possible that the balance of power had shifted in the corporations' favor.

Zale stood up, and everyone turned to look at him. "Now we know where the corporations got the DNA that created the cyborgs, but we don't know how they got it, or what it all means. If the IAF had gone over to the corporations completely, the whole *fraxxing* galaxy would know about it by now. We're missing too many pieces of the puzzle to make any assumptions yet."

Lance chimed in. "We know one thing for certain. If anyone involved with this Vault of the Fallen finds out we know what it was used for, they'll come for us. All of us. This is the kind of secret people kill to protect, so everyone needs to be damned careful from now on."

"I'm not afraid of the corporations," Royan declared.

"Which is another reason why you're headed to the Traffa system first thing tomorrow morning, little brother. If things go badly here, we're going to need you to tell the galaxy what's going on."

Royan opened his mouth to argue and shut it again when his sister skewered him with a look that would make a stampede of Nantari rhinos stop in their tracks.

Zale cleared his throat. "I've got a friend I can contact and make some inquiries. He's an IAF officer. A colonel, actually. I believe we can trust him, but considering what's at stake, I want a consensus from the group before I reach out to him."

"If the IAF brass doesn't know what's going on, this news isn't going to sit well. Can we trust him to keep it to himself, or will he report this up the chain like a dutiful soldier?" Dirk asked.

"Scott Archer knows how to be discreet, and he also owes me a big favor. I think it's worth the risk. If anyone doesn't want me to do it, say so. This affects us all."

No one spoke.

"Alright. I'll get in touch with Scott."

The gathering broke off into smaller groups to continue talking, and Lance managed to work his way over to where Lieksa was standing with her boyfriends, Mack and Dash. He'd gotten to know her a little when she had dropped by to fix Huey. He already knew Mack and Dash, as they were his commanding officers at Corp-Sec.

"Hi, Lance." Unlike most people, Lieksa always knew which one of his siblings she was talking to. The only other person he had ever met who could do it was Alyson. It was one of the many things he liked about the doctor. She saw so much that other people missed.

"Hello, Lieksa. I wanted to thank you again for fixing up Alyson's droid. We were feeling really badly about breaking him."

Dash chuckled. "Yeah, we heard Blade took out the poor thing before it could even finish greeting you."

Lance lowered his voice. "Don't let Alyson hear you calling Huey an 'it.' She has decided it's a he, and she gets annoyed if you use the wrong pronoun."

Mack blinked. "But it's a machine."

Lieksa poked her massive boyfriend in the ribs. "Some people said the same thing about cyborgs, and you are most definitely not an it."

"Damn right I'm not. And if you're ever in doubt, I'll be happy to demonstrate all the ways I'm a man."

Lance managed not to laugh, but it wasn't easy. Mack was a hardass to work for, but apparently, he was a lot mellower when Lieksa was around. He could understand that. He and his brothers were the same way when it came to Alyson.

Lieksa blushed and shook her head. "Behave yourself."

Dash snickered. "And where's the fun in that?"

She deliberately turned away from her boyfriends and smiled up at Lance. "So, how's the protection gig going? Is Alyson coping okay with everything?"

"That's what I wanted to talk to you about. Between the work she's doing and the need to keep her safe and secure, I think she's going a little stir crazy. In fact, I know she is. We've invaded her home and her workspace, and she can't escape. I was wondering if you or Zura might have a suggestion. We can't go to the Nova Club, or anywhere else she'd normally go."

Lieksa brightened. "I think I have the perfect solution."

By the time she finished explaining her idea, Lance thought it was perfect, too. It was exactly what they all needed, a chance to have a little fun.

"You're brilliant. Thank you." He gave Lieksa a brief hug, very aware that both Mack and Dash were glowering at him the entire time.

"Hands off. Your woman is over there. You want hugs, get them from her," Mack grumbled.

"Yeah. You three have already cost me my bet in the pool because you're moving slower than molasses in zero-g," Dash added.

"Well, now you have inside info. Use it wisely. I'm going to let my brothers know the plan. Thanks again, Lieksa. You really are brilliant."

He left the trio and went in search of his brothers. They had a lot of planning to do before tomorrow night.

CHAPTER SEVEN

Alyson knew the guys were planning something, but she had no idea what it was. They'd been acting like kids with a secret since the meeting last night, but they refused to give up any details other than the fact they were taking care of dinner.

She had spent the morning in the med center, looking in on her patients and staff. The highlight of her day had been when Nya had come in. The cyborg's badly mangled hand and arm were completely healed, with nothing left but a few scars that were already fading. Lieksa had done a remarkable job of repairing her cybernetic components, and Nya's medi-bots had taken care of the rest. After losing the overdose victim, Alyson had needed the win.

The afternoon had been dedicated to working on the cure to cyborg infertility. True to her word, Zura had tracked down everything Alyson needed. The last of the materials had been included in her brother Royan's last run, and he had delivered them himself before returning to his ship for the trip to the Traffa System. Before he left, Alyson had slipped a data stick with a copy of all the information they had loaded onto it, into his hand. If something happened, he would make sure that the information was passed on.

"It's done?" Lance asked.

"I think so. I've got a bunch of tests to run before I can be sure, but I believe this will work."

"How long until you know for sure?"

"If everything goes right, we'll know by mid-afternoon tomorrow." She gestured around the lab, indicating all the machines and computers hard at work.

Lance held out his hand to her. "Then it's time to celebrate. Come with me."

She took his hand and let him draw her in close. "We shouldn't celebrate yet. I don't know if it worked. What if I jinx it?"

"You won't jinx anything. You've earned some downtime, and we're going to see that you get it." He leaned down and brushed a feather-light kiss to her lips.

She leaned in, expecting him to kiss her again, but he withdrew instead.

"When I kiss you next, I don't plan on stopping. So, I think we should head upstairs, grab my brothers, and head out before I decide to lock the door and keep you all to myself tonight."

"If you tried to do that, I suspect they'd kick the door down."

He cupped her cheek with one hand. "You're probably right. We're going to have to figure that part out eventually. We all want to spend time with you, together and individually. Once the threat is gone, and we're not camped out at your bedroom door every night, we'll talk about that."

A few days ago, she was looking forward to having her home to herself again. Things had changed, though. When they left, she would miss them.

"The way things are going, you might be staying with me for quite some time. We're no closer to figuring out who left the warning in my office, and the number of potential enemies we're making keeps going up."

"Worried?" he asked, his hand still on her cheek.

"Of course, but not as much as I should be, all things considered. It helps to know that I've got the three of you watching over me. To be honest, I worry more about you and your brothers. You're the ones determined to put your lives at risk to protect mine."

"Don't worry about us, sunshine. We're exceptionally hard to kill."

"Why do I get the feeling that's a confirmed fact and not a cocky theory? I thought the three of you were never in combat?"

"You don't spend three years roaming the galaxy—especially the places we wound up—without running into trouble now and then." Lance winked, then reached down to take her hand. "If you come with me without any more questions, I promise we'll spend dinner telling you about all the times we got into trouble. And for the record, it was almost always Blade's fault."

She laughed and interlaced her fingers with his. "I bet he'll claim it was yours and Dirk's."

"Of course he will. And he'll be lying through his teeth."

They left the lab, and she took care to activate the entire spectrum of security measures, ensuring that no one else could enter the lab. It was sealed up tight and would stay that way until she came back to find out the results of her tests.

There was nothing else she could do tonight. Lance was right, it was time to relax and celebrate a little.

* * * *

When they arrived upstairs, Dirk and Blade were waiting for them. They had changed out of their red Corp-Sec uniforms, and both of them were decked out in pure black outfits. They were also wearing long, black leather coats, which seemed odd considering the entire station was climate controlled. "Are we going somewhere cold?"

"No, but we are going out, and that means we're carrying a few more weapons than the average citizen might feel comfortable with." Dirk opened his coat to reveal he was a veritable arsenal, including a knife, a blaster in a thigh holster and another one at his hip.

"Holy *fraxx*. Unless dinner is in the middle of a battlefield, I think you guys might be doing the overkill thing again. Are we going on a date or to a war?"

"This isn't overkill, this is being prepared. If we had packed the plasma grenades, that might have been over the line," Blade said.

"Oh, no. You do not have grenades in my house, do you?" They better not have brought explosives anywhere near her med center or she'd toss the grenades, and possibly them, right out an airlock and watch them float away.

All three of them laughed. "Just ignore him, Aly. We don't have anything like that. We're not suicidal. Explosives are fun, but they're not exactly a smart thing to have on a space station. One mistake and kaboom, no more Astek Station."

"I'm glad to hear even you have limits." She eyed their heavily armed forms and forced herself to remember that this was for her safety. "Do I get to know where we're going yet? I need to change, and it would be nice to know what I should wear."

The three of them looked at each other without saying a word, and she quickly realized they were talking to each other via their private comm channel.

"I swear, the next thing I'm going to work on is a way for us normal humans to hear your private conversations. I'm adding this to the list of things I think are rude."

"Sorry. Some habits are hard to break." Lance squeezed her hand, reminding her that she hadn't let go of it, yet.

"With everything going on, there aren't many places we could go that would be secure, so we came up with an alternative plan," Dirk explained.

"He means that I came up with a plan, and they recognized my brilliance and agreed to it," Lance interjected.

"Which still doesn't tell me where we're going."

"Think picnic. Nothing fancy. You look gorgeous in everything, so pick something comfortable and meet us out here when you're ready." Lance leaned down and kissed her cheek. "I'm going to get ready, too. Tonight is about relaxing and enjoying ourselves. I promise you're going to enjoy what we have planned. Leave the details to us, okay? You've earned this."

Dirk and Blade swooped in and kissed her, too, Dirk claiming one cheek while Blade pressed his lips to her brow before they both moved away again.

The kisses were all sweet and gentle, but her head was still reeling as she made her way to her room. This was it. She was going on a date with all three of them. *Veth,* if a few simple kiss made her giddy, what would happen when the four of them came together, and the sparks between them finally ignited?

She showered and changed in record time, picking out an outfit that she hoped would work. It was a bright yellow summer dress that she purchased the last time she was back home on Cassien Alpha to visit her grandparents, and it had been hanging in her closet ever since. It was the only thing she owned that fit with a picnic theme, though she still had no idea where they were taking her. The only spots she knew that might work were all far too open and insecure for the guys to have chosen.

The butterflies in her stomach were in full flight when she stepped out of her room. Dirk was waiting for her in the hall, and his eyes widened in male approval as he raked his gaze over her.

"You look stunning."

"And you look dangerous. And maybe a little sexy."

"Only a little? I thought women liked the dangerous, bad boy type?"

"You're a lot of things, Dirk Trello, but I don't think anyone would ever call you a boy." The three of them were pure male, a fact Alyson was acutely aware of every moment they were together. They were sinfully sexy, heartstoppingly handsome, and wrapped in an air of danger that made her brain turn to mush. Not that she was admitting that to them.

Dirk snorted. "I have never been, and never will be, a boy. And no one better call me that if they wanted to keep breathing." He offered her his arm. "Shall we?"

When her hand touched his arm, she felt a sizzle of heat that wound its way down her spine and pooled between her legs. Desires she'd done her best to deny awakened and added their flames to the fire kindling inside her. She drew a slow breath in an attempt to clear her mind, but it didn't work. "Let's get this date going…wherever you're taking me."

"It's somewhere all of us can relax for a while."

"That would be nice. You three have been on duty non-stop since I told you about the warning. You need this break even more than I do."

"It's not the break I'm looking forward to. It's spending time with you."

* * * *

Dirk kept Alyson tucked between himself and Lance as they made their way to their destination. Blade walked a few steps in front, choosing their path carefully as they wove through the crowded causeway. It wasn't likely they'd be attacked this soon after emerging from hiding, but they weren't taking anything for granted. They couldn't.

It wasn't until they stepped off the mag-lift that Alyson figured out where they were taking her. There was only one place on the station where the ceiling arched in a dome overhead, the metal hull plating painted to mimic the blue skies of a world most of the residents had never seen.

"This is the residential level Mack, Dash, and Lieksa live on. I've been here before. Is that where we're going, to have dinner with them?"

"We're not having dinner with them, no. But we are going to their home," Lance clarified.

"Please tell me that they know we're coming."

"Give us some credit. We may not have perfect manners, but we're not barbarians." Lance glanced at Blade. "Well, not all of us."

"You're going to pay for that at some point. Don't think I'm not keeping score."

"No fighting." Alyson's voice dropped to a soft murmur. "At least not unless I get to watch."

"You'd watch us fight?" Blade asked.

"So long as you weren't trying to kill each other, of course I would. I've got a standing invitation to attend every cage fight match at the Nova Club. They like having a doctor around in case something goes wrong. Not that it goes wrong very often. The Nova's fighters are well trained and know what they're doing."

"Now you've done it," Dirk muttered.

"We could take her to Corp-Sec headquarters. That's a safe enough place. Show her around, do some sparring in the gym," Blade suggested.

"I seem to remember someone blew up your HQ last month," she reminded him, shaking her head at the same time.

"Only part of it," Lance held up two fingers less than an inch apart. "It was a really small bomb."

"Still not convinced. I'm grateful for a chance to get out of the medical center, but maybe we should stick to visiting places that haven't had security breaches."

"By that criteria, you shouldn't be allowed in your office anymore, Doc." Blade's joke fell flat. It was a reminder to all of them that despite an extensive investigation, they still knew nothing about who had broken into Alyson's office to leave the warning. All Corp-Sec's efforts to determine where the threat might come from had failed, too. They were operating in the dark, and that fact haunted Dirk every hour of the day.

They made the rest of the journey in silence. It wasn't until they were almost to their destination that Alyson spoke up. "You told me tonight was about relaxing and enjoying ourselves, and that's what we're going to do. The second we walk through those doors, we're going to put all of this aside for a few hours. Agreed?"

"Agreed." One of the most fascinating things about Alyson was her ability to say just the right thing to set those around her at ease. She was a true empath, reading people's moods in a way he couldn't even begin to understand. His upgrades allowed him to interpret body language and read micro-expressions humans couldn't even detect, but he still didn't understand others the way she did. She amazed him in so many ways.

Lance went up to the door and entered the security codes, spoke a voice command, and set his hand down on the scanner to verify his identity. Only then did the door open, letting all of them enter.

"So, where are our hosts?" Alyson looked around in confusion.

"At the Nova Club for the evening. Come on, we still have a little way to go yet." Lance pointed to an almost unnoticeable door.

"They gave us their house?"

Lance entered another access code and the door slid open, revealing a staircase. "They loaned it to us for a few hours. You've been stuck in the med-center for days, and this is one of the safest places on the station. We've arranged for a Corp-Sec transport to get us home, too. In case anyone saw you leave."

"So, we have this whole, amazing place to ourselves, and we're going to the basement?"

"Trust us," Dirk said.

Her hand tightened around his. "With my life."

It was the highest compliment he had ever been given. When words failed him, Dirk did the only thing he could think of to show her what it meant to him. He pulled her into his arms and slammed his mouth down on hers. Need tore through him. He didn't simply want her, he craved her. The heat of her mouth, the slender lines of her body pressed against his, the soft moan that reverberated against his lips as she gave herself over to him.

After a lifetime spent as an outsider, adrift, distrusted, and feared, she gave all of them the one thing they yearned for: acceptance. In return, he'd happily give her everything he had to offer. Even his life.

"Uh, Dirk? This date would go a lot better if you let go of our girl long enough for us to actually arrive," Blade pointed out with a note of impatience.

"Before you let go, I have a question. What was that for?" she asked.

He stared down into her soft gray eyes and finally found the right words. "For being you. No one else sees us the way you do."

"And how do they see you?"

"Outsiders," Lance answered.

"Dangerous," Blade said.

"Unworthy."

"You're none of those things. Not to me."

"And that's why we're falling in love with you."

Dirk had no idea which one of them had spoken. It didn't matter. All three of them knew it was true. It wasn't until he felt the weight of three surprised gazes that he realized he'd been the one to utter the words.

Alyson didn't say anything, and her face was an unreadable mask. His brothers were staring at him like he'd grown a second head. *Yeah, this is going well.*

When she started to laugh, an icy hand wrapped itself around his heart and started to squeeze, but then she stroked his cheek and smiled. "You really don't have a subtle bone in your body, do you?"

"Not really." He leaned into her touch and thanked the stars above she understood. It was one more reason in a very long list why she was the perfect woman for them.

"Don't change." She looked around at the three of them. "I'm starting to like it."

* * * *

Alyson was so distracted by Dirk's confession that she didn't pay much attention to where they were going. Stairs. Walls. Desks. It looked like an office of some kind. Lance was punching a code into yet another keypad when she finally took a good look at the pictures and notes that covered the walls. There were lists of corporations, rosters of names, some of which she recognized as cyborgs that lived on the Drift. There were images, too. "Hey, those are from outside my office door. And is that the forensic report on the weird pyramid message I got?"

"You've been busy working on your own projects, so you've never been down here." Blade gestured around them. "Welcome to our group's headquarters, or as Lieksa likes to call it, the bunker."

"Good name for it." She started to walk toward the nearest wall to get a better look, but Dirk caught her hand, stopping her. "We're not here to work, remember?"

"We're here, for this." Lance stepped aside as the door slid open, revealing an impossible vista.

A meadow of blue-green grass and wildflowers lay on the other side of the threshold. Even standing where she was, she could hear the twittering notes of birds singing.

"How? What?" She rushed to the door and peered inside. The illusion—it had to be an illusion—was even more amazing up close. The sky overhead was a familiar shade of pale blue, and the hills that rose in the distance were ones she had seen countless times before. This was Cassien Alpha, her home planet, and the scene in front of her was a stunning recreation of the area where her grandparents lived.

"How?" She asked again.

"Apparently, our bosses are rich enough to have an entire sim-suite at their disposal. Lieksa helped us track down a program with data from your homeworld, and we recognized this area as similar to the one you have projected on your wall." Lance cocked his head toward the door. "You going to go in? Or are you going to stand and stare at it?"

She kicked off her shoes and stepped into the sim. Her bare toes sank into the soft grass, and a light breeze swirled around her, making her dress flutter around her knees. Even the scent of the flowers was exactly the way she remembered it. A green and silver butterfly rose from the meadow to dance in the air in front of her, and she chased after it, just the way she used to do as a little girl. She forgot that it was an illusion and ran in the sunshine, letting go of all the dark worries and fears that had taken root in her soul over the last few months.

Footsteps pounded up behind her, and she spun around to see all three of her men running toward her, grinning and hooting with laughter as they raced across the field.

She squealed and broke to the left, leading them a merry chase for as long as she could. It didn't take long for them to catch her. A pair of strong arms wrapped around her and lifted her high into the air as her captor crowed in triumph. "Got you."

"Yes, you do. The question is, what are you going to do with me?" She managed to twist enough to see that it was Lance who had caught her.

"That's a loaded question. You sure you're ready to hear the answer?"

There wasn't a doubt in her mind. Not anymore. "Yes."

"You two are in charge of organizing dinner. I'm taking our date on a tour," he called out to his brothers.

"You've got ten minutes, then we're coming to join you. Meet you by the pool?" Blade asked.

"There's a pool?" she asked.

"Uh huh. Want to take a pre-dinner dip with me?"

"I didn't bring a swimsuit. No one mentioned that was a possibility." And she might not have believed them if they had told her. Even now, surrounded by the interactive hologram, it was hard to wrap her head around what she was experiencing.

Lance cradled her in his arms, then lowered his head to brush a kiss across her lips. "That was intentional. I've never been skinny dipping before, but I hear it's fun. Want to try it with me?"

She laughed. "You're trying to get me naked? Now? I thought we were having a dinner date."

"Damn right I'm trying to get you naked. I don't care about dinner. I want you, Alyson. I want to strip this pretty dress off and devour you, then carry you back to the others, lay you out like a banquet, and spend the rest of the night showing you what it's like to be loved by three men at once."

Her heart started to hammer against her ribs, and a frisson of heat danced over her skin. "I want that, too."

He groaned, lifted her high enough to kiss her again, and started jogging across the meadow, sending a cloud of jewel-colored butterflies rising into the air.

It was a magical, wonderful moment that should have been perfect, but she was haunted by a faint, nagging voice reminding her that moments like this always came with a price.

By the time they arrived at the edge of a brook-fed pool of crystalline water, her stomach was twisted into knots. Amid all the fear and chaos of her life, she had finally found something good to hang onto. Lance, Dirk, and Blade were more than her bodyguards, they were her strength. Almost everyone she had opened her heart to had hurt her. If she did this and they walked away from her, she wouldn't just be hurt, it might cost her everything, including her life.

"You're frowning," Lance said softly. "Why?"

"I… it's…" She gave an embarrassed huff and decided to be honest. "I'm worried about what will happen if I stop fighting this and give in."

Lance stared into her eyes as he lowered her gently to the ground and held her close.

"What do you think is going to happen?"

She shrugged and blushed a little. "I don't know. I think that's the problem. This is uncharted territory for me. I only trusted one other man the way I trust the three of you, and it didn't end well."

"What happened?"

"He cheated on me. We were engaged to be married, and I found out he'd had a mistress for almost the entire time we'd been together.

He made a strangled choking noise and shook his head. "So he was an asshole and an idiot?"

Her embarrassment faded a little, and she nodded. "Pretty much."

"Anyone who cheated on someone as amazing as you doesn't deserve to have you in their life. And for the record, if you left us, that wouldn't be the end of anything. We'd follow you. Across the Drift or the *fraxxing* galaxy, for as long as it took to convince you we belong together."

"That's sweet. And a little scary. I think there are a few laws about stalking someone you should probably read up on."

He chuckled and nuzzled her hair. "Probably. You know what I mean, though, don't you?"

"I think so." She understood, but that didn't mean it was easy for her to accept. Not once in her life had anyone come after her. Every time she had walked away from the people who were supposed to love her, they'd let her go without a fight.

"Don't think. Feel." He touched a hand to her chest, right over her heart. "Right here."

Alyson closed her eyes and laid her hand over his. "I haven't followed my heart in a long time. You're going to have to show me the way."

CHAPTER EIGHT

Lance had never seen Alyson like this; vulnerable and unsure. They had been so busy enjoying the chase, it hadn't occurred to any of them to wonder why she had held them at arm's length for so long. Now, he could see the truth, and it made his heart ache. Someone had hurt her, leaving her tender heart scarred and wary.

He wrapped an arm around her waist and bowed his head until their mouths were only a whisper apart. "I can't lead you somewhere I've never been. We'll have to find our way together."

Her only answer was a gentle sigh as she swayed against him, and he finally gave in to the need that had driven him for weeks. His mouth claimed hers in a searing kiss that sent his senses spinning. She tasted sweeter than any fruit he'd ever savored, and he knew he would never get enough of her. Not her sweet taste, or the subtle notes of her perfume, or the way her body fitted against his. This was why he had waited so long to kiss her - because once he had her in his arms like this, there wasn't a force in the universe strong enough to make him let her go.

His brothers were still within view, arranging the food and wine they had brought on a blanket stretched out among the flowers. They would be joining the fun soon, but for this one, sweet, delicious moment, he had Alyson all to himself.

The two of them were wrapped around each other, but despite the challenges, he managed to shed several layers of clothing and weapons without letting go of her. It wasn't until he began pulling off his shirt that she started to help. Her soft fingers glided over his bare skin, across his chest and then down, following the waistline of his pants until her hands were stroking up and down his back. When his shirt hit the grass, he turned his focus to her.

"Tell me there's an easy way to get you out of this dress or I might just tear it off of you."

"No need to get violent. The zipper's in the back."

"Then all I need is your permission. Do you want this, Alyson?"

She smiled up at him, her lips swollen from his kisses and her eyes full of trust. "Yes. I just hope—

He cut her off with a kiss before she could finish her sentence.

He pulled her in tight, letting her feel the hard length of his cock as he rocked his hips and ground their bodies together. His fingers found the zipper of her dress and tugged at it until it stopped midway down her back. Her warm skin was bare beneath his hands, their tongues tangled, bodies melded together from thigh to chest.

A light shrug and the straps of her dress slid off her shoulders, a slight wriggle and the entire dress began to slide downward. She let go of him long enough to let the dress fall to the ground, and then she was back in his arms again, blushing and naked except for her panties; which were nothing more than a scrap of fabric and lace that hid very little.

The sunlight played over her pale skin, highlighting every dip and curve of her slender frame. He wrapped a handful of her shining hair around his fingers and tugged her head back before kissing his way from her mouth to the exposed lines of her throat. Her hands splayed across his chest, and her hips rocked in time to his. He tore his mouth from her flesh to look around and quickly spotted the perfect location to continue their tryst. Lifting her again, he carried her to an outcropping of smooth, sun-warmed rocks near the center of the pool. He gritted his teeth as the water rose to his thighs. The cool water did almost nothing to quench the need burning inside him, but it did help to clear his head a little. Too bad it came too late to remember he was still wearing his pants...and boots.

"Did you forget something?" She was giggling.

"I got distracted. See what you do to me? A couple of kisses and I'm walking into lakes with my clothes on."

"That might be the most flattering thing anyone has ever said to me."

"That's me, master of flattery."

"So, now what, oh master?" She gestured around them. "And don't you dare think about dunking me."

"The last thing I want is for you to cool down, sunshine. In fact, I think it's time I turned up the heat."

He set her down on the flattest of the stones so she was sitting about a foot above the water. She let go of him and settled herself carefully into her new throne, reclining back on her hands and letting her toes dangle in the water.

She looked stunning, like a water fairy or a mermaid from an old Terran folktale. He tore open his pants and leaned in to kiss her, working his way slowly downward from her lips to the perfect rise of her breasts. He couldn't keep his hands off her. There was so much of her he wanted to stroke and savor. He moved slowly, enjoying every second of exploration until she was moaning and trembling beneath him.

"You are gorgeous," he whispered, and sank down. She blushed and moved her legs closer together, but he stopped her, setting his hands against her inner thighs and pushing back until she stopped resisting.

He eased her legs apart until he could fit his shoulders between her knees, and only then did he remove his hands and reach for the knife still strapped to his thigh. He had her panties cut off before she had time to protest, and he winked at her as he stuffed the ruined garment into his pocket.

"You aren't keeping those."

"Oh yeah, I am. I'm thinking of starting a collection."

"You're going to be buying me replacements, then."

His cock went harder than hull plating at the idea of buying her underwear. Lace and silk in every color and cut he could find. "That's a brilliant idea. We'll buy them, you can model them, and then one of us can tear them off and add them to the collection."

She laughed. "Well, I guess I know what to get you all for your birthday and any other holiday, then."

"*Fraxxing* hell, yes please."

He dropped one shoulder and eased her leg over it, then did the same on the other side so her knees were over his shoulders and he was caught between her thighs. She was still blushing when she reached for him, her fingers tangling in his hair as she drew him in closer. "I think that's my line."

"Huh?" he muttered, barely able to think anymore.

"Whatever it is you're going to do. My answer is, yes, please."

He groaned, turned his head to kiss the soft skin of one of her inner thighs, and then moved in to press his face against the slick lips of her pussy. The heady scent of her arousal filled his senses, and he parted her lips with his fingers, exposing the delicate pearl of her clit. He lapped at it with the tip of his tongue, and she arched upward, crying out with delight and surprise.

That note of delight told him everything he needed to know about her past lovers. They hadn't known how to please her, and he relished the knowledge that he could be the one to show her what she'd been missing. Well, he'd get to start her education, and then the three of them would give her a scorching demonstration.

*

Alyson was acting like a shameless wanton, and for the first time in her life, she didn't care. Lance's mouth was magic, and every touch of his tongue made her ache for more. She was so lost in her pleasure that she didn't hear Dirk and Blade arrive. It wasn't until one of them hissed at the chill of the water that she opened her eyes and saw they weren't alone anymore.

"You had to take her into the middle of the damned pond?" Dirk grumbled.

"And you left your pants on. Alyson, sweetheart, please don't judge us all by the actions of this idiot. I promise you, we're smarter than him." Blade appeared at her side and leaned in to kiss her as Dirk vanished behind her before she could see more than a glimpse of his hard, and very naked body.

"Hello, gorgeous." Dirk wrapped his arms around her, and she leaned back to nestle against the broad bulk of his body. His hands smoothed up her sides to cup her breasts, the calloused pads of his thumbs stroking over her nipples until they tightened into hard points.

"I thought you were on dinner duty?" she asked.

"We were. Then we heard you moaning. Did you really think we'd stay away after that?" Dirk asked.

Lance raised his head from between her legs for a brief moment to mutter. "I was hoping you would, yeah."

Blade snickered. "Not a chance."

Distracted by the three sets of hands caressing her, Alyson didn't say anything at all. She didn't have enough focus left to form words. Lance bowed his head again, and she moaned as he zeroed in on her clit, working it with his tongue and teeth until she felt herself trembling on the edge of exquisite release. She crossed her ankles behind him and lifted herself up, silently urging him on.

Blade and Dirk were taking turns claiming her lips and blazing a trail down to her breasts.

"Are you ready to come for us, Alyson?" Dirk whispered, his lips brushing against her skin with every silken word.

She managed to moan and nod her head despite the heat that flooded her cheeks.

Lance uttered a muffled laugh that made her entire body hum with pleasure as the vibrations rolled through her.

"Show us how good you feel right now. Let us hear you. I can see you're close. So close."

Blade closed his teeth on her nipple, making her gasp as a bolt of something that wasn't quite pain zinged straight to her clit. Her pussy walls tightened, and Lance slid two fingers into her channel, pushing her over the edge and into orgasm.

Her senses exploded as her orgasm bloomed and rose up to consume her, carrying her away on a wave of sensations that left her limp and gasping for breath.

"Watching you come was even sexier than I'd imagined." Lance sounded utterly smug as he rose up from between her legs and grinned at her.

"You're incredible," Blade declared a split second before he kissed her so deeply her toes curled and she forgot to breathe.

By the time he released her from that kiss, Lance had moved to her side, and Dirk was standing in front of her, one hand wrapped around the thick length of his cock as he eyed her with blatant hunger.

"Yes?" he asked, and there was a multitude of meanings locked into that single word.

She swallowed sharply. This was it. If she said yes, then everything changed. She hesitated, but then realized she was lying on a rock, naked and still trembling from an amazing orgasm. Things had already changed—for the better.

"Yes." She nodded.

Blade chuckled from somewhere behind her. "Good answer."

She tipped her head back to look at him, and Lance groaned. "Perfect. Stay just like that."

"Oh, yeah." One of the others spoke, but she wasn't sure who. Right now, it didn't matter. They were all in this together.

Lance cradled her gently, his arm across the back of her shoulders so that her head fell back toward Blade and she was supported a few inches above the rock she was lying on. Dirk gripped her hips and moved between her legs. He drew her legs around his waist, and she gasped as his cock pressed against the still sensitive folds of her pussy. Her head starting to buzz from all the blood rushing to it and she felt a brief flash of doubt. Could she really do this?

Lance leaned in close and nuzzled her ear. "Don't think. Feel."

She closed her eyes tried to relax.

Dirk rocked his hips, dragging the thick head of his cock across her pussy and then covering her clit with the pad of his thumb. He caressed her with fingers and his cock, teasing her with promises of pleasure to come. Something soft brushed against her lips, and she opened her mouth, her tongue sweeping out to taste what was being offered to her. The scent of musk and the salt-tangy taste of pre-cum. She opened her mouth wider, using her tongue to swirl delicate circles around the head of Blade's cock.

They fell into a languid rhythm of give and take. Each stroke and caress moved her back and forth, while Lance held her safe between them, whispering encouragements and a litany of lurid descriptions of what was happening around her.

By the time Dirk finally seated himself at her entrance, she was more turned on than she'd ever been in her life. Consumed by desires she couldn't even name, she met Dirk's gentle thrust with one of her own, driving him deep into her body.

"I think she's done waiting," Lance chuckled, his breath still a soft buzz by her ear. "Tell us what you need, Alyson."

"More. I need more. Please." She barely recognized the broken, breathless words as hers.

"From both of us?" Blade asked.

She nodded and reached up to grasp his shaft in her hand, guiding it to her mouth and drawing him inside. All three men groaned, and then everything seemed to go up in flames. She was filled at both ends, mouth and pussy, cocks stroking in deep and then withdrawing again, as Lance stroked and toyed with her breasts with his free hand. She was caught in a maelstrom of needs and desires, all of them working together to scale the highest peaks of pleasure, reaching levels of bliss she never even dreamed of.

Blade uttered a low growl of need and tangled his fingers into her hair as he pushed deeper into her mouth. She flattened her tongue against the top of his shaft, using it to stroke and tease.

Dirk's hands tightened on her hips as his thrusts became shorter and harder. Every stroke passed over nerve endings alight with new sensations, and soon she was quaking with need, desperate for a release that she couldn't quite reach.

"I've got you, lover," Lance murmured, and she followed the touch of his fingers as they trailed down her stomach, not stopping until they pressed against the throbbing flesh of her clit.

She moaned and arched herself higher, pushing Blade's cock deeper into her throat.

Instinctively she reached for Lance, her fingers finding his cock and wrapping around its thick length.

"*Veth*, woman. You don't have to…"

She couldn't speak, but she tightened her fingers around Lance's cock until he stopped arguing. She wanted to be connected to all of them, giving them each as much pleasure as they were giving her. Hand, mouth, pussy, they claimed her together, and it wasn't long before it all became too much, and she moaned loudly.

"Perfect," Dirk groaned.

"So perfect," Blade echoed his brother's sentiments.

"Ours," Lance pinched her clit on Dirk's next thrust, and she fell into an orgasm so powerful the world went dark, and there was nothing but wave after wave of breathtaking bliss.

She was roused by the primal cries of her lovers as they came in turn. Hot cum filled her body, flowed down her throat, and covered her midriff as she took them over the edge with her.

Too satiated to even move, she let herself drift in a hazy fog for a while. Something cool and wet stroked her thighs, her stomach. She opened her eyes as Lance lifted her into the air, carrying her back to shore.

"You know if you keep pampering me this way I might decide to never let you stop."

"You've figured out our cunning plan," Blade said, appearing beside her. He was still naked, and it dawned on her that she was, too. Suddenly embarrassed, she shrank in on herself, hands covering her breasts as she drew her knees in tighter.

"Don't," Lance murmured, then raised his voice so that his brothers could hear every word. "You are gorgeous and amazing, and your ex-fiancé was a *fraxxing* idiot to cheat on you. Never doubt that for a minute. Being with you made all three of us lose our damned minds. That's how amazing you are. Do you believe me?"

A quick glance around revealed that all three of them staring at her, waiting for an answer. After what they had shared, there was only one answer she could give them. "I believe you. I'm already trusting you three with my life. I might as well trust you with my heart, too."

Dirk's cautious expression melted into a smile and Blade winked at her. "Another good answer."

She stopped trying to hide and reached out to her lovers, instead. They took her hands, and they walked back through the meadow together. It felt so right, she regretted spending so much time trying to keep them at a distance. These were the men she needed. Blade, who could always make her smile no matter how tired or stressed she was. Lance, who always knew the right words to make her feel better. And Dirk, her stubborn, steadfast lover who spoke from his heart. This was where she was supposed to be. Surrounded by men who cared for her, and would do everything in their power to keep her safe.

CHAPTER NINE

Blade slipped out of bed the next morning without waking Alyson. She was still curled between Dirk and Lance, sleeping peacefully. Her blonde hair was sleep-mussed, and while there were still shadows under her eyes, they were less noticeable than they'd been in weeks.

"Coffee?" Lance's query sounded inside his head.

"On it. Maybe breakfast in bed for our sleeping beauty?" Blade sent back.

"Maybe you're not the dumb one, after all," Dirk said.

"We all know that I got the looks and the brains."

He left the bedroom as silently as he could and stepped into the hall, moving around the neatly folded stack of blankets and pillows Alyson insisted on leaving out for whoever was assigned to guard her door as she slept. Last night would have been his turn, but instead of sleeping out in the hall, Blade had fallen asleep with Alyson in his arms. It was how he hoped to fall asleep every night from now on.

Huey already had the food dispenser working on coffee by the time Blade arrived in the kitchen. The droid kept the kitchen well stocked with food, did the laundry, and somehow managed to keep up with the mess he and his brothers made. After living in a constant state of disarray and chaos, it was far too easy to get used to the way Alyson lived.

None of them were quite sure how she afforded it, though. The medical center wasn't cheap to run, and she paid her staff generously. Even assuming her spacious living quarters were included in the exorbitant fees she paid to Astek Corporation for her lease, she still lived a very comfortable life for a young doctor with no business partners. There was still a lot they didn't know about each other, but time would change that. Now she had finally dropped her guard, anything was possible. All they had to do was protect her, and her research, until it was time to tell the galaxy the dirty secrets that the corporations were doing their best to hide.

Ten minutes later, he was carrying a tray loaded with coffee, pastries, and assorted breakfast options, while Huey followed a few steps behind, carrying an even larger tray and two folding contraptions they could set the trays on.

"Did you bring the whole kitchen with you?" Dirk asked in a hushed voice as they re-entered the bedroom. He was eyeing the trays with amusement.

"Huey and I couldn't decide what to bring, so we brought a little of everything."

"Aw, you're bonding with the bot. You finally made a friend," Lance jested.

"It's too early in the morning for you three to start with the brotherly banter," Alyson declared in a raspy voice as she stretched beneath the covers. "What's my rule?"

"No banter before coffee or Alyson gets grumpy." Blade rattled his tray. "In my defense, I did bring the coffee."

She cracked open one eye and grinned as she extended her hand to him and wriggled her fingers. "You're now my favorite. Gimme."

"You're adorable and far too easy to bribe. Might I suggest setting the bar a little higher?" Dirk leaned in to kiss her cheek, careful not to jostle her newly acquired mug of coffee.

"What do you suggest?"

"For starters, a massage every morning," Dirk said.

"Followed by breakfast in bed," Lance added.

"And of course, coffee and orgasms, in whichever order you'd prefer," Blade concluded.

Alyson spluttered into her coffee, and when she looked up again her cheeks were pink, but she was smiling. "That's quite a morning routine."

"We're full-service bodyguards, Doc. And we're all yours."

Dirk rose to help serve breakfast, and Blade claimed his place on the bed. "Whatever you need. All you have to do is ask."

Her eyes gleamed with pure contentment, and her smile was bright enough to put the stars to shame. "Right now, I have everything I need right here. This is the nicest wake up I've ever had."

It was the nicest morning he could remember, too. Since Alyson had come into their lives, everything was better. It was a sappy sentiment he would never admit aloud, but it didn't make it any less true.

While they ate, the conversation flowed from topic to topic until she asked a question they'd never been asked before.

"Why are the three of you so different? I thought the corporations used clones because it made sure that you all acted and thought the same way. You three don't. Not really."

All three of them looked at each other, then back at her. "You're the first person to notice."

"Then no one else is paying attention. Luke and Kit are a lot more similar to each other than the three of you." She tipped her head to one side. "I'm assuming it has something to do with the fact you were released from your behavior modification programs right away."

"That's part of it," Dirk said.

"And the rest?" she prodded softly.

Dirk spoke for all of them. "Most places we signed on to work didn't need three bodies to do the same job. We wound up doing different tasks, and learning from different people. There were stretches of time we barely saw each other. We all developed our own skill sets."

"And developed your own personalities, too. I mean, it's obvious you three are related, but I don't understand how anyone could miss the differences between you."

"I told you before, sunshine. No one else sees us the way you do."

Blade leaned in to steal a coffee-flavored kiss. "What Lance said."

She cradled her coffee in her hands, staring down into the mug as if it contained the secrets of the cosmos. "So, what do you see when you look at me?"

"A beautiful woman who is so far out of our orbit we shouldn't even be breathing the same atmosphere," Dirk said.

It was a truth none of them had spoken out loud until now. She was sexy, fierce, cultured, and smarter than all three of them put together. As determined as they had been to win her over, Blade still wasn't sure how in the galaxy they had gotten so lucky.

Alyson's head jerked up. "Don't say that. I'm not too good for you."

"Yes, you are, but that doesn't matter. You're ours now, and we're not letting you go." Blade recognized the expression on their lover's face. It was a mixture of self-doubt, denial, and yearning.

He knew the feeling well because he'd lived with it for years.

"There's still a lot about me you don't know."

"So? You'll tell us when you're ready. There's a lot you don't know about us yet, too," Dirk said.

Blade snickered. "You make it sound like we're fascinating and complicated. We're not." He pointed to Dirk. "That one's bossy. Lance likes to watch, and I'm an extroverted flirt. Lance likes to tinker with machines. I play chess, and Dirk is a hell of a bartender, but he can't dance. At least, not as well as Lance and me. There you have it, the Trello brothers summarized."

"You can dance? Where did you learn that?" she asked.

Dirk and Lance groaned.

"I thought we swore never to bring that up again?" Lance reached past Alyson to swat Blade's shoulder.

Blade ignored him and winked at Alyson. "Ask me again sometime, and I'll tell you all about our brief but glorious stint as exotic dancers."

"You stripped? Where? Was it on the Drift? Wait, does this mean I'm officially dating ex-strippers? Phae is going to be so proud of me. She's always telling me I need a little adventure in my life."

Dirk pinched the bridge of his nose and shook his head. "I tended bar on this misadventure. My minimum standards for employment are higher than these two lunatics."

"We were broke, and it seemed like a good idea at the time. Yes, it was here on the Drift. And yes, you're dating a couple of former exotic dancers. As for adventure, I think you've got more than your share of that right now. When Phae gets here, she's going to be amazed at how much trouble you've managed to find."

Alyson actually grinned at that. "You know, you're right. For once, I think I'm in more trouble than she is."

"And you're happy about it, too. *Veth*, woman, what are we going to do with you?" Dirk asked.

She drained her mug and handed it to Lance and then stretched back out on the bed, eyes shining above her blushing cheeks. "I do believe someone mentioned orgasms and coffee, and I'm all out of coffee."

* * * *

Alyson was humming to herself as she punched in the security code of her laboratory door. She felt better than she had in months. Contentment had softened the sharp edges of her worries, and she had finally slept a deep and dreamless sleep undisturbed by nightmares or fretful awakenings that left her staring at the ceiling for hours.

She bounced on her toes as the system deactivated and the door finally unlocked. She started to rush in, eager to see if her tests had worked, but Dirk's hand landed on her shoulder and held her in place.

"Us first," Dirk chided her.

Blade stepped past her and into the lab. "Red lights are bad, right?" He asked a few seconds later.

Cursing, Alyson ran into the room, not caring about safety protocols. Three steps into the room, it was clear something had gone wrong. Red lights flashed on almost every console, and several pieces of equipment were completely powered down. Her tests, the samples-- Everything was ruined. "What the *vething* hell happened?"

Lance appeared beside her, draping a comforting arm around her shoulders. "What could have caused something like this?"

"Stay with Alyson. I'm going to check the security footage. I'm locking the door behind me. Stay sharp," Dirk ordered before leaving, his heavy footfalls echoing down the corridor.

Taking a deep breath, she forced herself to let go of her emotional response and focus on diagnosing the problem. Like any of her patients, she couldn't fix anything until she knew what had caused it, and why.

"I think it was a power fluctuation. It might have even been a localized blackout. I'm still guessing, but it looks like everything here lost power sometime last night. The powered-down equipment is all the most delicate stuff, the ones vulnerable to power surges."

"Are you saying it was sabotage?" Blade asked. He had

"I don't know. Is that even a possibility? The station's power supply is heavily protected. It has to be," she mused.

"Every system has its vulnerabilities," Lance sounded more solemn than she'd ever heard him.

"The med-center is supposed to have redundancies to stop this sort of thing from happening. Independent power supplies and stuff. This—" she gestured around her. "Shouldn't have happened."

"Can you redo the tests?" Blade was still holding her gently, his thumb moving in calming circles across the top of her shoulder.

"I can. I'll get started right now. It'll go faster if you two help. I'll show you what to do."

Lance nodded, but Blade shook his head and jerked his head toward the door. "I'll stand watch. Dirk's right. We need to be on guard."

"Can one of you contact Mack or Dash and let them know that the tests failed and I need to re-run them? They can let Cynder know there's been a delay. "Damn it. I really wanted to give her good news." She sighed and tried to push past her bitter disappointment. How could she even begin to apologize for failing Cynder and the others?

"And you will have good news for her. Soon." Blade changed direction and came to stand in front of her. He bent his head down, nuzzling her cheek before stealing a kiss. "Cyn and the others know you're doing your best. This isn't on you, Doc."

The door to the lab opened, and all three of them spun around. Dirk stood there, his hands clenched into fists and his green eyes stormy. "Blade's right. This isn't on you. This is on us." He tossed a data tablet onto the nearest counter and pointed to it.

"What's this?" she asked.

"Your shielded friend was back late last night. While we were distracted upstairs with you, he was roaming the med-center."

The tablet showed a single, frozen image of the same blurred figure, only this time he was standing outside the laboratory door instead of her office. The hairs on the back of her neck rose. She had managed to push all thoughts of her strange stalker to the back of her mind. It was easier not to think about it, but now he was front and center in her mind again.

"I don't understand. Why warn me last time, and then sabotage the work he told me to finish?"

"Does it really matter why?" Dirk was almost snarling with frustration as he jabbed a finger at the screen. "He was here again, and we had no idea. He's a *fraxxing* phantom."

Lance came over to stare at the tablet. "Tell me we know how he got in and you've already got the tracking software running."

"It's running. Cocky bastard waltzed through the front door."

"How can you track someone that doesn't show up on sensors?" Alyson asked.

"That tech uses a lot of power. Corp-Sec can detect the power consumption and track it. It'll only work when the shield is activated, but if we're lucky, we can follow the route he took."

Blade joined them. "And if we're really lucky, the bastard will have made a mistake and let himself get caught on surveillance somewhere before or after he shielded himself."

She frowned, feeling like she was missing something. "Then why don't we have those energy tracking things in here? We'd know if he came back."

"We tried. It's not common equipment, and what they have is hardwired into the station," Lance said.

"And even if it was available, there's too much equipment in here that would interfere with it. Diagnostic computers, lab equipment, and scanners. This place is full of gear that would give false positives." Dirk shot her a dark look. "I don't suppose you're ready to talk about moving somewhere more secure?"

"You know I can't do that. Not until I've synthesized a working cure. You've made it clear that coming and going is too risky to do again, so I need to stay here and finish this. When it's done, maybe all four of us can go away together. I think we'll have earned a vacation by then."

"Say the word, and we'll pack up and meet you at the docking bay of your choice," Blade said.

"A vacation sounds good," Lance agreed.

Dirk picked up the data tablet, then looked straight at his brothers. "We're not on vacation, yet. We need to up our game. Lance, you stay and help the doctor. Blade, watch the *fraxxing* door. I shouldn't have made it into this room when I walked in here the last time. Do better. The doctor's life depends on it."

He was gone before she was over the shock of what he'd just said and done. He'd talked down to her and barked at his brothers like they were lackeys. "What was that?"

Blade's upper lip curled in distaste. "Dirk at his grumpiest. Charming, isn't he?"

"Don't worry about him, sunshine. His bad mood will pass."

She nodded and got to work resetting the machines and adding new samples. Lance might have told her not to worry, but she couldn't help it. It wasn't Dirk's anger that bothered her, though. It was that he was pulling away. She hadn't missed the way he had referred to her as 'the doctor,' and what happened between the four of them last night was a hell of a lot more than a mere *distraction*. How had they gone from confessions of love and a passionate night in bed together to this? It was what she'd been afraid of; opening her heart only to have it broken again.

By the time she had all the tests running again, her mood was as dark and cold as the void outside the station's hull. There were no more jokes with Blade, no flirty moments with Lance, and when she got back to her office, she found the paperwork on her overdose victim sitting on top of the pile. Michael Vons. Yet another person she hadn't been able to help.

She sank down into her chair and uttered a low sigh. She felt as if she was letting everyone down these days. The temptation to contact Phaedra and make sure she was alright was strong enough to have her reaching for her comm device, but she stopped before picking it up. She couldn't take the chance. She couldn't risk talking to Phae in case it gave away her location. Her friend was in enough danger already thanks to the favor she had done for Alyson.

She glanced up at Lance, who was leaning against the wall, arms folded over his chest and his eyes fixed on the door to her office. He was lost in his own thoughts and about as much company as the cup of yesterday's coffee, which still sat on the edge of her cluttered desk.

She ignored the pang of loss that tugged at her heart and started on her paperwork. Clearing away the stack of work would at least let her feel like she was accomplishing something.

* * * *

Dirk knew Alyson was unhappy, but he couldn't allow that fact to distract him from what he and his brothers needed to do. They'd lost focus once, and it had come with a cost. It wouldn't happen again. Alyson was too important. Too many people were relying on her. He loved her, but it would be selfish to put his feelings ahead of everything else. First and foremost, they needed to protect her. When this was all over, they could take that vacation Alyson had mentioned. All of them together, with no need to be on guard, and no chance of losing the woman who had won their hearts.

The evening passed in relative silence. No one spoke much, and even Huey seemed less chipper than usual as he went about his chores. After dinner, they usually played a game or two of fortress chess, but not tonight. The chess board sat unused on a side table. It required four players, and the new plan he and his brothers had worked out meant they weren't together anymore. One of them was with Alyson at all times, while the others stood watch at strategic points. Tonight, Blade would guard her bedroom door while he and Lance stood watch at the only entrance to her quarters. They had called in reinforcements from their team at Corp-Sec to patrol the medical center below.

They wouldn't sleep again for days, but it was a small price to pay for the added security. Nothing was going to happen to Alyson or her precious research.

"Your friend Phaedra should get here tomorrow. Do you want me to talk to my boss about getting her a security detail of her own?" Dirk asked, breaking the silence that had gone on since dinner.

Alyson barely looked up from her data tablet. "No need. She's going to stay at the Nova Club. They can protect her there. She'll love the bar, it's her kind of place. Free booze, good food, and all those hot fighters for her to flirt with."

"You didn't tell me you'd taken care of that already. I could have arranged something."

"You've already got your hands full protecting me. Since you seemed to want to focus on that, I dealt with Phaedra. It wasn't difficult. Cynder was more than happy to set it up."

Her words were neutral, but her micro-expressions and cool tone made it clear that she was angry and upset.

"Your safety is our primary mission right now, but if there's anything else we can do for you, you know you can ask, right?"

"Yeah, I know." She lowered her head and started reading again, letting her hair fall around her face to act like a screen she could hide behind.

"Alyson…" he spoke her name, not sure what he was going to say, but he needed to say something. He would step in front of a pulse rifle blast for her, or take down a host of enemies with his bare hands to keep her safe, but he had no clue how to deal with this situation. Weapons and tactics were his skill set, not feelings.

She didn't answer him. *Fraxx.* This day had started out so well, but then they'd been reminded of the danger circling them, waiting for them to make another mistake. Dirk had failed to protect her once. There was no way in hell he would do it again. No matter what it cost him, Alyson would survive.

CHAPTER TEN

Alyson went to bed early. She could use the extra sleep, though thinking about why she hadn't slept the night before made her heart ache. Last night had been wonderful. Tonight, things were about as far from wonderful as they could get.

All three of her lovers were quiet and withdrawn. They were keeping their distance, and it made her feel even more isolated. She understood the logic behind the changes. It was her life being threatened, so she could appreciate what they were trying to do. That didn't stop it from hurting, though.

I should never have dropped my guard. This would be easier if we had never been together.

Crawling into bed only made her feel worse. It felt too big and empty with only one person in it, and when she snuggled under the quilt, she could still smell their scent lingering on the fabric. She turned off the light and closed her eyes, but her mind wouldn't stop whirling. Even the smallest noise caught her attention, and after half an hour she sat up again. "Computer, lights, middle setting."

There was a gentle rap at her door, then Blade asked, "You okay in there?"

She shot an irritated look at the door as if he could see her expression somehow. She didn't want the reminder that one of the men missing from her bed was on the other side of the wall, listening to everything that went on in her room. Not that anything was going on tonight apart from insomnia.

"I'm fine. Not having much luck sleeping is all."

"I can have Huey brew you some tea if you want."

A frustrated sigh escaped her lips before she could stop it. "Tea isn't what I need right now. But thanks for the offer."

Silence for a few seconds, followed by a surprising offer. "Would you like me to come in for a few minutes? I could stay with you until you fell asleep."

She wanted to say yes, but asking for Blade to join her felt too close to begging.

"I thought you were avoiding any and all distractions?" she asked.

The door slid open, and Blade stormed through, looking decidedly annoyed. "You're not a distraction. Don't you ever say that again."

"Then why are you all treating me like I'm a thing to be guarded from a distance? There wasn't any distance between us last night, and I felt safe." She knew she was acting childishly, but she couldn't help herself.

He sat down on the bed beside her and hauled her into his lap, dragging the quilt and blankets with her. "Because the first time we dropped our guard, that asshole showed up and *fraxxed* with your research. What if he'd come after you instead?"

She leaned back so she could meet his gaze. "Then he would have come into this room and found me protected by three big, naked, cyborgs who would have cheerfully torn him to pieces."

"Unless he got the drop on us. Your stalker has a *fraxxing* shield, and those aren't supposed to be available to the public. Who knows what else he's got in his bag of tricks. As much as it pains me to admit it, Dirk's right. Protecting you has to be our first priority."

"I hate this. I understand, but it feels like..." she sighed and hid her face in the crook of his neck instead of finishing her sentence.

"I don't like it either. *Fraxx*, none of us are happy about this. Do you really think Dirk and Lance want to be standing guard tonight instead of being here with you?"

"Honestly? I wasn't sure. It would have been nice if one of you had said so," she said, her words muffled against his skin.

"I'm saying so, now. I know it's a little late, but in our defense, we've never had anyone in our lives besides each other until now." Blade tapped his temple. "We usually know what each other's thinking at all times. It saves us from having to talk about feelings and stuff."

She smiled a little at that. "Feelings and stuff, huh?"

Blade nodded. "This is all new, and really, It's your fault that the timing is so bad. If you had just said yes the first time we asked you out, then we'd be further along in our learning curve. But no, you had to wait until your life was in danger."

"I was afraid of what would happen if I let you into my life," she confessed.

He tangled his fingers into her hair and tugged at it until she lifted her head. "And I was afraid you were never going to let me in."

"I didn't think you were afraid of anything."

He lowered his mouth to hers and whispered, "The only thing I'm afraid of is losing you." She leaned in to kiss him, needing to show him how much his words meant. She closed her eyes and let go of everything but the happiness she felt at being back in his arms. This felt right. No, it was better than that. It felt like she was falling in love.

Blade kissed her with bruising passion, his every touch demanding a response as his mouth slanted across hers. He tossed aside the blankets, and before they had finished hitting the floor he was working the oversized shirt she wore to bed over her head while still trying to kiss her. She laughed, and so did he, and then she was naked in his lap.

"That's better," Blade whispered against her throat as he dusted a slow, leisurely trail of kisses down the side of her neck.

"Much better." She slipped her hands under his shirt. She wanted to touch bare skin, to connect with him in every way.

The trail of kisses continued lower until his lips brushed one pert nipple and he sucked it deep into his mouth. One hand was splayed between her shoulder blades, supporting her as she leaned back, giving herself over to him.

"Open for me."

She didn't understand what he wanted at first, but then he stroked along the top of her thigh, and she parted her legs.

He gave her nipple a light nip, sending shockwaves straight to her clit. "Ouch."

"Good ouch or bad?"

Heat flooded her face as she considered her answer. "More good than bad."

"I love how you blush every time we talk dirty to you. It makes me want to tell you every wicked, depraved thing that comes to mind."

"You wouldn't."

He lifted his head and flashed her a wicked grin that made her pulse race and her pussy grow slick with need. "Say that again."

"You wouldn't talk dirty to me just to make me blush, would you?"

"You have no idea the things I'd do to you if you'd let me." His next kiss was savage, possessive, and hotter than a solar flare. His fingers slid into her pussy as his tongue tangled with hers. Her gasp of pleasure was lost in the heat of his kiss, and his groans rumbled against her lips as his hips jerked upward, grinding their bodies together.

She kissed him back, keeping her eyes open as they came together in one blistering rush of need and heat and lust.

He used just one finger, flicking it back and forth across her clit. When she finally tore her lips from him to take a deep breath, he let his gaze wander down her body.

"You are so damned beautiful like this. Naked and breathless and curled up in my lap. Do you have any idea how many times I imagined getting you like this?"

She shook her head.

"So many nights I've lost count. I'd lie in bed and imagine all the things I wanted to do to you. Tasting your skin, playing with your gorgeous breasts until you were squirming and begging me to suck them. I wondered what you would taste like and how you'd feel when I finally got to fuck you."

His words turned her on, and she couldn't hide it, not when he was watching her so intently and his fingers were inside her.

"Do you want me inside you again? Now?"

She nodded. "I—I do. Yes. Please."

He uttered a low groan and nuzzled her cheek, then withdrew his hand and lifted her off his lap and back onto the bed. "Don't move."

She reached for the blankets, but there wasn't anything to cover herself with. The bedsheet and quilt were still lying in a heap on the floor.

Blade finished skinning his shirt over his head and skewered her with a look that made her pulse race. "You moved."

"I—" she pointed over the edge of the bed to the pile of bed linens.

"Don't need anything but me to keep you warm. And if you were thinking of covering up one inch of your glorious self, think again."

His eyes started to twinkle as he looked around the room. "Computer, activate reflective surface mode on all walls."

"What?" panic and a thrill of something much more intriguing coursed through her as she caught on to what Blade intended.

"Trust me. This is going to be fun." He stripped off the rest of his clothes as she watched. His reflection was captured on every wall, letting her admire him from multiple angles. Okay, maybe this wasn't a bad idea, after all.

*

Blade was fighting a battle to stay in control. He didn't want to rush this, but seeing her lying on the bed, flushed, naked, and waiting, was enough to push him to the breaking point. He wasn't supposed to be in her bedroom at all. They'd agreed that they had to focus on her protection for now, but when she had called herself a distraction in that bitter, pained tone, he had made a judgment call. What good was protecting her body if they ended up causing her a different kind of hurt?

"Since I'm not supposed to move, I think that means you have to come to me," she said with a soft laugh.

It wasn't until she spoke that he realized he'd been staring, his feet rooted firmly to the floor. His cock was painfully aware of the separation, however. It was hard, throbbing, and pointed in Alyson's direction. Every cell in his body vibrated with need as he made his way to her side, crawling into bed and drawing her into his arms again.

He watched their reflection as they kissed. She looked fragile next to him, her slender body and soft curves dwarfed by his massive frame. There were so many times he'd resented how he'd been designed. His bulk and strength ensured he could never blend in anywhere. He dealt with fearful whispers and resentful stares everywhere he went. Even on the Drift, there were some who were deeply biased against the cyborgs. But not Alyson. She had never looked at him that way. Her lovely figure was wrapping for an even more beautiful soul.

"Lie on your side, back to me," he instructed her between kisses.

She obeyed him with only the slightest hesitation, but that shadow of doubt was back in her eyes when he next saw her face in the mirror.

"You're thinking too much."

"So, distract me."

He settled in behind her, pressing his cock to the lush curve of her ass as he fitted their bodies together. He slid a hand between her thighs, coaxing her to lift a leg up and over his so that her pussy was visible and she was on display in the mirror across from them.

"I don't know about you, but I'm very damned distracted right now." He let his fingers glide over the top of her thigh and down to her pussy, stroking along the seam and parting her damp curls.

"Mmhmm."

"Do you want my fingers inside you again, Alyson? Do you want me to fuck you until you come all over my hand?" Her eyes widened at his crude words, but her legs parted a little more, and she rocked her hips against his hand.

"Is that a yes?"

She blushed again and whispered, "Yes."

With a low groan, he buried his face against her neck, sucking on the delicate skin at her throat as he pushed his fingers into her channel. A flood of moisture flowed over his hand, and her inner walls gripped hard around his fingers, making his balls tighten and his dick turn to stone. Soon, he wanted to feel those tight muscles clamped tight around his cock instead of his fingers.

He pumped her pussy with slow, deliberate strokes, keeping his thumb on her clit as he primed her body for an orgasm.

"That feels so good. Don't stop. Please don't stop."

"I'm not stopping until you come for me. Then I'm going to fuck you until you come again. I've got you all to myself, and I intend to enjoy every second of it." He would have to answer for it later, but right now, he didn't give a damn. She needed this, and so did he.

Shifting his hand slightly, Blade pressed his fingers deeper into her tight passage, curling them slightly as he sought that sensitive spot that could push her over the edge. She flexed her upper leg slightly, lifting herself as she instinctively helped him in his quest.

The second his fingertips found their target, her entire body stiffened, and she moaned his name. She was trembling in anticipation, eyes bright as their gazes met in their reflection. She was enjoying watching this as much as he was. He worked her clit harder and faster as his fingers hit the sweet spot again and again. He wanted her to come so hard that she remembered this night forever.

The finale came quickly, hitting hard and leaving her breathless and quaking in his arms. She was still panting as she reached over her shoulder to lay a trembling hand on his cheek.

"I never imagined..." she trailed off and nodded toward the mirror.

The look on her face did wonders for his ego, and his chest swelled as he saw the slight indent where her teeth had closed on her lower lip as she came.

"I know, I'm amazing," he winked at her in the mirror.

"Yeah, you are." Stroked his cheek. "I'm a very lucky woman."

"I think you got that backward. We're lucky to have you, Alyson. We're three broke, broken drifters who haven't had much luck in our lives, not until you came along."

They were interrupted by shouts and heavy footsteps in the hallway outside. Alyson paled as the door slid open and Dirk came charging in, a blaster in his hand.

"You weren't at your post!" Dirk bellowed.

"He was with me because I asked him to keep me co—"

"You left her unguarded so you could score some time in bed? What the *fraxx* were you thinking?" Dirk cut her off with an angry slash of his hand.

"Back off, Dirk. You're scaring her." Blade was torn between his desire to punch his brother in the face and the need to shield Alyson. She was tense and shaking in his arms, and he didn't want to let go of her to teach Dirk a lesson.

"He's not scaring me. He's pissing me off!" She tore out of Blade's arms and stormed across the room to plant a finger in the center of Dirk's chest. "Don't you dare come into my bedroom yelling and waving a firearm ever again."

"I thought you were in trouble. Did you want me to stand out there and politely knock while someone killed you?" Dirk snapped.

Lance charged into the room at that moment, and Blade wanted to laugh at the jumble of expressions that crossed his face as he took in the scene in front of him. An angry, naked Alyson, glaring at Dirk, the bed was a wreck, and Blade was still naked. *Oops. He should probably do something about that.*

"Everyone okay?" Lance finally asked, holstering his weapon.

"No." Alyson had calmed down enough to remember she was naked and stomped back to the pile of blankets to fish out her t-shirt and put it on, tossing Blade his clothes at the same time.

"You could have sent me a message," Blade tapped his temple and shot both his siblings a death glare as he pulled on his pants and tucked the rest of his clothes under his arm.

"Right back at you. You know you weren't supposed to be in here. We made an agreement." Dirk finally put his blaster away, but he didn't look any calmer.

Alyson made a noise strangled noise of frustration. "And that's the problem. You made an agreement about me, without talking to me. I know you want to keep me safe, but I get a vote in how that happens. Blade knew I was upset and he was trying to help me feel better. He was also trying to explain why you were all acting like last night never happened."

"We have to protect—" Lance started to speak, but this time it was Alyson who interrupted.

"I don't want to hear that word again. In fact, I don't want to hear from any of you right now. Everyone, get out." She pointed to the door.

"All of us?" Blade didn't want to leave her. Not now, when she was clearly upset.

She flashed him a tiny smile, but her eyes were dark and stormy. "All of you. I'm sorry."

"Don't be sorry. This is not your fault." Blade knew exactly whose fault this was, and he was going to kick his ass once they got out of earshot.

"I'll see you in the morning." She looked over at Dirk. "And I meant what I said. If you walk into my bedroom again with a weapon in your hand, I'm done."

She was retreating from them already, and it wasn't only physical distance. Even Dirk seemed to have calmed down enough to realize he'd screwed up because he didn't argue with her.

"Next time, I'll knock," he said before leaving. Lance looked like he wanted to say more, but in the end, he blew Alyson a kiss and followed Dirk into the hall.

"To be continued," Blade said. "If you need me, I'll be on the other side of the door, thinking about you."

* * * *

He went for Dirk the second Alyson's bedroom door closed, slamming his fist into his brother's stomach and throwing him up against the nearest wall. He didn't want Alyson to overhear this conversation, so he opened up a channel between the three of them.

"What the fraxx *was that? Are you trying to ruin the best thing to ever happen to us?"*

Dirk's response rang inside his head like someone had dialed the volume up to maximum. *"I'm trying to keep her alive. Maybe you should have been thinking the same thing instead of getting laid."*

"Asshole," Blade growled out loud and shook Dirk hard enough to make his head snap back, striking the wall.

"What the hell did I miss?" Lance demanded.

"Dirk lost his mind, and we might have very well lost Alyson because of it. You gave me shit for tackling a droid, but you charged into her bedroom with a blaster in your hand, bellowing like an enraged Torski."

Dirk shoved him hard in the chest, forcing Blade to step back and release him. *"Blade left his post. I was going to ask him if he wanted a cup of coffee or something to eat, and he wasn't where he was supposed to be. I assumed the worst and ran into*

Alyson's room and well, you saw how I found them. Naked and totally distracted."

Lance groaned and squeezed the back of his neck as if trying to stave off a headache. He looked over at Alyson's door and then back to the two of them. *"So you went to console her, and your clothes suddenly fell off? You should have told us you were with her. I understand the motivation, but..."*

Blade knew they had a point, but he wasn't ready to admit it. Not to them, at least. *"Can we focus on the bigger problem and save the lecture for later? Alyson is not just an asset to protect. She's the woman we love. Hell, Dirk said the words last night. You can't tell someone that and then shut down and pull away the next fraxxing day. She's hurt and confused right now. She thinks we're pulling away from her, and the way we're acting, who can blame her?"*

There was a long stretch of silence as all three of them pondered the situation.

"Shit," Dirk eventually muttered as his shoulders slumped, and his head bowed almost to his chest.

"We were programmed for combat and asset protection, not this." Lance looked pained, and a little lost as he leaned against the nearest wall.

"Then you better figure it out, fast." A new, but familiar voice interjected.

"And while you're at it, you should probably figure out which comm channel is which," someone else added with a snicker.

"*Mack? Dash?*" Blade said, though he already knew the answer. They weren't linked to anyone else, and he still wasn't used to being connected to anyone but his brothers. As angry as he was, he hadn't paid attention to which channel he'd opened. Wonderful.

Both of his brothers rolled their eyes and muttered under their breath.

"*Since you've already heard everything, got any advice?*" Blade asked.

Dash snickered again. "*Yeah, if you're done growling and snarling at each other, we can probably help. Dirk and Mack have a lot in common. He nearly screwed things up with Lieksa by being an overprotective idiot. Since we're awake, thanks to you, why don't we drop by? We can give you the crash course on all the ways you're going to fraxx up this relationship, and what your best moves are for fixing it afterward.*"

"*We could bring along some of the others, too. They've been doing this longer than we have.*" Mack suggested.

All three of them groaned.

"It's an intervention," Lance muttered.

"Maybe that's what we need. Apparently, we're not doing so well on our own." Dirk didn't look thrilled at the prospect of sharing his feelings with a bunch of other men.

Blade was right there with him, but for Alyson, he'd give it a try. "*Bring whoever you think can help, but be quiet about it. Alyson's asleep, and we can't leave her unguarded."*

"I'm insulted. Do you really think anyone is going to go after her with a bunch of cyborgs between them and her room? Not to mention our team members are patrolling downstairs. Your phantom would have to be insane to come anywhere near that place tonight. We'll see you in thirty minutes and give you a heads up before coming upstairs. If you shoot any of us, I'm demoting you," Mack replied.

Blade returned to his post outside Alyson's door, then said to the others in a low voice. "Tell me when they get here. And you better activate Huey. He's going to be thrilled to have so many guests to take care of."

"I'll get him started on food prep right away," Lance said.

Dirk stayed where he was until Lance was gone. "We good?"

"Yeah. She makes us all act a little crazy sometimes. That's why we need to fix this."

Dirk nodded. "Do you think I'd be doing this for anyone else?"

"She's worth it," Blade agreed.

"Things have sure changed since we came to the Drift. Six months ago it was the three of us against the universe. Now, we've got jobs we like, a woman we love, and friends who are willing to show up in the middle of the night to help us." Dirk smiled. "Can you believe it?"

"Not really. But even if this is all a dream, I'm ready to fight to hang onto it for as long as we can."

CHAPTER ELEVEN

Alyson woke early and rushed through her morning routine. She wanted to grab a fast bite of breakfast and head downstairs as quick as possible to check on the lab and her test results. If they were good, then she was finally going to be able to give Cynder and the others some much needed good news.

Blade was on his feet and beaming when she walked into the hallway. His upbeat demeanor was a far cry from how she felt after the events of last night. Not that she was letting herself dwell on that. Over the course of her life, she had gotten good at setting aside hurt feelings in order to focus on what needed to be done, and she had important work to finish. "You look a lot happier than the last time I saw you."

"That's because I've been looking forward to doing this." And with that, he pulled her into his arms for a toe-curling kiss. She pressed her hands against his chest, trying to push him back, but she'd have better luck trying to shove a planet out of its orbit.

"Do you want me to stop?" he asked, barely moving his head away enough to be able to speak.

"You need to let go of me. I can't do this. Not right now. It's better for everyone if we have a little distance, right? Then I'm not a distraction, and you three aren't fighting with each other."

He moved back just enough to be able to look into her eyes. "Doc, we talked about this already. Brothers fight, it's what we do. And you are not a distraction. You're the woman I love, and I want to be the first one to apologize for not handling this better."

Words failed her. Blade was apologizing. He had even said he loved her. The walls she had spent all night rebuilding came crashing down again, leaving her heart vulnerable.

"Doc?"

She bit her lip as an emotional tug-of-war raged inside her. "I've been on this roller-coaster ride once already. I don't want to ride it again."

"It's not going to be like that. After you went to sleep, we got some things figured out. We're going to do better in future." He gave her a lopsided smile. "If you're willing to give us a second chance, that is."

"Before I agree to second chances, maybe we should go find the others." She reached up on tiptoe to kiss his cheek. "But that's for making this morning better than I thought it would be."

"What in starsfury happened here?" she asked, the second they walked into the kitchen. Huey was bustling around, stacking dishes and sorting silverware, and there was enough food set out to feed half the Interstellar fleet. "Are we expecting company?"

Dirk looked sheepish as he handed her a mug of fresh coffee. "They left about an hour ago. Sorry about the mess, we were hoping to have it cleaned up before you joined us. Oh, and good morning."

"Uh, good morning to you, too. Care to elaborate on the company comment? Last thing I heard the plan was all work, no play, and protect Alyson at all costs."

"Believe me, last night's company was all about you," Dirk said before stepping back to let Huey zip past.

"And it wasn't play, either." Blade snagged a sandwich off of Huey's tray. "Shall we get out of here and leave the droid to finish cleaning up?"

"Good idea," Lance started loading a plate with a variety of food. "We can tell her all about the impromptu intervention while we eat. I've got yours here, sunshine, you go sit down."

Bemused, she wandered to the table and sat. Did she fall into an alternate dimension while she was asleep? Or maybe she was still dreaming. What the *veth* had happened last night?

She sipped her coffee and waited until her lovers joined her at the table. Lance's long hair was still damp from his shower, and both he and Blade had trimmed their beards since the last time she'd seen them. Dirk was freshly shaven, and all three of them were wearing fresh clothes.

Ignoring the plate of food in front of her, Alyson cut straight to the point. "What intervention? Who was here?"

"Mack and Dash came over to give us some advice," Dirk said.

"And he brought Toro, Jaeger, Kit and Luke with him for backup," Blade muttered into his juice.

"Well, that explains the amount of food lying around and the mountain of dishes." She gestured to the three of them. "I still don't understand what changed, though. I thought we weren't supposed to be all together like this anymore? You wanted to put some distance between us. Me asset. You bodyguards. No more distractions."

Dirk rose from his chair and rounded the table to crouch beside her. "That was a stupid idea, and I'm sorry I ever suggested it. I'm regretting a lot of things this morning, but most of all, I'm sorry that I hurt you. It's been explained to me by those with more experience in these matters that the best way for us to protect you is to be with you instead of pushing you away."

Understanding dawned, along with a slow kindling flame of hope. She'd been there for the aftermath the night Lieksa had stormed out on her boyfriends for being overly controlling. Lieksa had come to Alyson for advice, and they had all ended up at the Nova Club for a girl's night out. Zura and

Cynder had shared some insight into dating cyborgs and the challenges of polygamous relationships. Apparently, this time it had been the guys turn to step in and help.

"And while we're making apologies, I owe you one, too," Lance reached across the table to take her hand. "I'm sorry. We should have talked to you about this instead of reversing course without any warning."

She looked around the table at the three of them, all solemn-faced and sincere. The tiny flame of hope burned brighter, and she took a leap of faith. She wanted to believe this was still possible. That *they* were still possible.

"Apologies accepted. And I should offer up one of my own, too. I should have told you that I was upset instead of shutting down. I let my past experiences with relationships and my family dictate my reaction."

Dirk leaned into her side and let his head rest against her shoulder. "Feel like telling us about that?"

"There's really not much to tell. My parents are…let's just say they're very important to their community. They were, and still are, influential people with a lot of demands on their time. I was always competing with everyone else for my parents' attention. I'd do almost anything I could to please them. My former fiancé, Bryce, was one of those things. He was someone my parents encouraged me to date, the son of a friend of my father's. I was trying to appease my family, so I agreed to go out with him."

"Not much of a reason to start a relationship," Dirk said.

"No, it wasn't. But he was sweet, and charming, and attentive. For the first time in my life, I didn't feel alone. I was certain he'd forget about me while I was at medical school, but instead of calling it off, he proposed after my sophomore year. I was over the moon. There was finally someone in my life I could trust. When he suggested I consider dropping out of school to marry him, I actually considered it." She sighed. "I was a fool."

Blade scowled. "Did you love him? Because from what I'm hearing, it doesn't sound like he was worthy of you."

That was a question she had asked herself often. "I fell in love with him, yes. I was a lonely girl who wanted to be loved. Being with him made my parents happy, and that meant they paid more attention to me. They thought he was a great catch. He was from an influential family with money and the respect of the community. I was their only daughter, and they had a lot of expectations for me." She uttered a dry laugh. "I've managed to be a spectacular disappointment to them in almost every way."

"How the *fraxx* could you possibly be a disappointment to anyone?"

Lance looked so outraged at the idea of her disappointing anyone, it made her wonder what it would be like if she ever brought the three of them home to meet her parents. *Re'veth*, she could probably sell tickets to that event. Her mother's parents would love them, though. They were the only ones who had encouraged her to find her own path, no matter what the consequences. They were the reason she was a doctor out on the Drift, and the only family she kept in regular contact with.

"My family is a whole other conversation, one that will require alcohol. My big brother joined the IAF when I was still a kid just to get away from them. I resented him for that for a long time, but now I get it."

Dirk stood, pausing to kiss her brow on the way. "Whenever you're ready to talk about it, we'll be here. For now, we should let you eat."

She dug into her meal with enthusiasm. Last evening she hadn't had much of an appetite, but today she was famished.

"I take it by the fact all of you are here and calm that my stalker didn't show up last night?" She asked between mouthfuls of her sandwich.

"Everything's quiet and secure. Some of our friends are still on watch, making sure no one gets through the front door, your elevator, or anywhere near the lab," Dirk said.

Once you're ready, we'll escort you downstairs and find out if you've got good news for Cynder and the others." Lance winked at her from across the table. "I think today is going to be a good day."

"I *fraxxing* hope so. I don't want to have to tell the others I let them down again." If the universe was feeling generous, today would be the day she finally got to fulfill her promise to Cynder. Giving the cyborg women back the ability to have children might be the greatest achievement of Alyson's life. It wouldn't have been possible without the help of her friends and her three loving protectors. They had done something no other man had ever done. They'd believed in her.

"I wanted to tell you how much it means to me that you've been here the last few days. You kept me alive, and because of you, we might finally be able to undo what the corporations did. However this ends, I just want you to know, I'm grateful."

"We'd do anything for you, sunshine," Lance said.

"I'm starting to realize that. It's going to take me a little while to accept it, is all." She smiled at them, hoping they could see in her expression what she wasn't ready to say out loud. Despite the rocky start, missteps, and random droid attacks, she was falling for them, fast.

* * * *

Lance let Alyson open the door to the lab and tried not to laugh as she begrudgingly stepped aside to let him into the room first. He did a quick sweep to ensure nothing was out of place, but all the equipment was where it had been yesterday, with not even a beaker out of place. This time, the machines were all still working, and he saw nothing but blinking green lights on their consoles. The extra patrols had done their job. No one had meddled with her lab overnight.

"It's clear."

She raced into the room like a kid entering a candy store, her eyes wide and a hopeful smile that got progressively wider as she went from machine to machine.

"It worked!" She did an adorable skipping dance around the laboratory, waving her hands in the air and cheering.

When she bounced past him, he swept her into his arms and lifted her into the air. She was so happy she glowed, and her joy was contagious. "Congratulations. You did it."

"*We* did it." She beamed down at him, then held out her hands to his brothers as they joined the celebration.

Dirk took her out of Lance's arms and swung her in a tight circle, careful not to knock any of the sensitive machinery that lined the walls. "How long until we can tell the others? How many more tests do you need to run to be sure?"

"I can tell them as soon as you put me down. Cynder's waiting for me to contact her. If I tell her I need her to come in for some bloodwork, she knows that means it worked."

Dirk was grinning as he handed her off to Blade, who kissed her before finally setting her down again. "Congratulations, Doc. You changed a lot of lives today. Your parents may not be proud of their amazing daughter, but we are."

Tears shimmered in Alyson's eyes as she pulled out her comm device and called Cynder.

It was a brief discussion, but by the time it was over Cynder's voice was quavering. "I'll be there soon," she said and signed off, but Lance could swear the tough as nails cyborg female was on the verge of tears herself.

Alyson rubbed her eyes with the heel of one hand and took a deep breath. "I've got enough prepared for one dose. That's for Cynder. Once I've given it to her, I need to come back here and start setting up to produce bigger batches. Zura's all ready to ship it out when there's enough, and once Phaedra arrives, she'll work with her connections to make sure the word goes out."

She looked around, looking dazed. "This is really happening."

Lance was at her side in a second to wrap a supportive arm around her shoulders and draw her in close to his side. "It's happening. Tonight, we're going to celebrate." He caught Dirk's scowl and added. "A small party, nothing too crazy. Once the danger has passed, we'll have to have a blowout at the Nova Club."

"Do you think I'll still be in danger once the cure is available and the word is out? That would be like locking the hangar door after the shuttle left."

"We can't be sure. And until we're certain you're safe, we're not taking any chances," Dirk declared.

No one was going to hurt Alyson, not while any of them still drew breath.

CHAPTER TWELVE

Cynder didn't arrive for her appointment alone. Tagging along behind Cyn and her two husbands, Jaeger and Toro, was a fuchsia-haired pixie who barely came to Toro's chest.

"Surprise!" Phaedra announced as she popped out from behind the pair of massive cyborgs and ran across the largest exam room to give Alyson a rib-creaking hug.

"Phae, you're here! You didn't tell me your ship had docked."

"That wouldn't be very stealthy of me, would it?" Phae's smile faded as she gave Alyson another squeeze. "And from what I've heard since I got here, I'm not the only one who needs to be staying out of sight."

"You told her?" Alyson asked Cynder. She had hoped to be able to explain everything in person. That would have let her spin things so that Phaedra didn't worry too much. Which was probably exactly why Cyn had updated the newest member of their little rebellion herself.

"Just the basics. What you've been working on, who might be after you because of it, and where Phaedra's information fits into the big picture."

Phaedra let her go and arched a hot pink eyebrow. "You've been holding out on me, Princess."

"Princess?" Blade asked, barely stifling his amusement.

He and his brothers were standing guard outside the examination room. They would have preferred to be inside, but there wasn't enough room. Med centers were designed for treating patients, not social gatherings.

"Don't you dare, Phae."

Phaedra chortled. "They don't know they're dating royalty?"

"Explain, please." Dirk's tone was a barely disguised demand, and Phaedra burst out laughing.

"You did not just bark an order at me, big guy, did you? I don't take orders well, just ask, Princess, I mean, Alyson."

Jaeger glanced over at Phaedra. "By any chance is your last name Watson? I swear you could be related to Zura and Royan."

"You noticed that, too, huh?" Blade grinned.

Sensing that things were veering out of her control, Alyson raised her voice. "We're here for Cynder, which means everyone who isn't Cynder, or married to her, needs to get out and let me work." She shooed everyone toward the door and hoped Phae didn't reveal her every secret while she was out in the corridor with her men.

Well, at least now she didn't have to see their faces when they found out who her father was.

* * * *

Dirk was having trouble picturing his elegant and quiet Alyson rooming with the tiny powerhouse of energy and attitude standing in front of him. From her bright pink and fuchsia curls to her scuffed and battered combat boots, Phaedra was the exact opposite of Alyson in every way imaginable.

Blade stepped in to do introductions. "It's nice to meet you. Alyson's told us about you, but since you've been out of contact, I'm betting you don't know much about us. I'm Blade, and these are my brothers, Lance and Dirk."

"The boyfriend bodyguards. Wow, where did she find you three?"

"Actually, we found her," Lance said.

"And we'll do whatever it takes to keep her safe. You've been briefed on what's going on?" Dirk kept his wording deliberately vague. While the staff were used to their presence now, they all believed the threat was from the Drojo cartel seeking revenge. They still had no idea what was really going on. That would change soon, but for now, the truth had to remain a secret. It was safer for everyone that way.

"Enough to know that she trusts you with her life." Phaedra's hazel eyes narrowed. "You better not let anything happen to her. She's one of the best people I've ever met."

"Nothing is going to happen to her. We'll make sure of it. Now, what's this about her being royalty?" Dirk had a feeling that whatever Phaedra was about to tell them, it would go a long way toward explaining why Alyson had fled so far away from her family.

"You know where she's from, right?"

"Cassien Alpha. It's a well-established colony planet. Lots of mining and resource exports." Dirk had looked it up, and Lance had learned a little more about the place when he was looking for a sim program for their picnic date.

"Guess whose father has governed the entire northern hemisphere of that planet for the last decade or so?"

Blade uttered a low whistle.

"Alyson's father runs a *fraxxing* planet?" Lance asked, stunned.

"Half of one, anyway. He's up for election next year, so who knows if he'll still be in power when it's over, but for now, yeah. She's more or less royalty on Cassien A."

Phaedra gave them a quizzical look. "You really had no idea? I mean, I know Alyson changed her last name after graduation, but it wouldn't take much to uncover her past. She doesn't hide it, she just doesn't talk about it much."

"We had no idea. All she's said is that she isn't close with most of her family and that explaining why was a conversation that would require booze. Now, I can see why." Phaedra's information answered some questions about Alyson but opened up a host of others.

"You said she changed her name when she graduated. Whose name did she take?

"She took her mother's maiden name. She's Dr. Jefferies, just like her grandmother."

"I think those are the only members of her family I ever want to meet. If we meet her parents, it might not go well." Lance muttered.

Dirk silently agreed. If they ever met Alyson's parents, they'd probably end up arrested for punching the planetary leader in the face and spend the rest of their life in prison. Alyson was an incredible woman, and it baffled him that her own parents couldn't see that.

Phaedra chortled. "They're going to lose their minds when they hear that Alyson's dating the three of you. I'm tempted to leak the info myself just so I can watch the reaction."

"I think Alyson's got enough to deal with right now without adding family drama to the mix, don't you?" Dirk reminded Phaedra.

Her face fell. "Right. I always said she was going to go rebel one day, but not in my wildest dreams did I figure it would be anything this big. I thought maybe a tattoo, or a boyfriend her parents would hate..." Phae snickered softly. "Though, looking at you three, I'd say she certainly nailed that one."

Muffled cheering came from inside the examination room, and they all turned to look, even though there was nothing to see but the dented, dull beige door.

"They sound happy," Blade observed.

Dirk lowered his voice to a whisper. "With good reason. What the corporations did to us, in general, was bad enough, but what they did to our women was unforgivable. Alyson is giving them back something precious."

All of them nodded, and even the exuberant Phaedra was subdued as they waited for the others to finish. This moment was going to have reverberations throughout the galaxy, and it had all started here, with a brave and possibly slightly insane group who had found the courage to defy the corporations. Dirk was honored to be among their company and blessed to be able to call them his friends.

*

Alyson was the last to leave the exam room. She took a brief moment to compose herself before rejoining the joyful throng that filled the corridor outside. Laughter wasn't a common sound for a place like this. They would have to go upstairs where they could celebrate properly, but not yet. She stood with the now empty vial of the cure in her hand. Her fingers, which had been so steady when she had injected Cynder only a few minutes ago, were trembling now.

"You okay?" Lance appeared in the doorway, the smile on his face contradicting the look of concern in his eyes.

She opened her mouth to say she was fine, then stopped and gave him a more honest answer. "I think it's finally sinking in. You know? I was so busy making this happen, I didn't have time to think about what it meant."

He walked over and pulled her in for a hug, his arms holding her close as he bowed his head to kiss the crown of her hair. "You changed a lot of lives today. Hell, you're the reason for a whole new generation of lives."

"And they'll all have their mothers' nanotech. What I've done is going to affect the future of the human race." She finally gave voice to the doubts that had started to whisper in her ear the moment the cure was in her hand. "Do you think I did the right thing?"

Lance didn't hesitate. "You did. And so did Zale when he offered the medi-bot tech to everyone in our group. That comet broke orbit when Kit and Luke injected Zura with their medi-bots to save her life. The technology was going to spread eventually. Once the corporations lost control over us, their creations, it was inevitable."

"But I'm the one—"

He completed her sentence before she could. "You're the only one smart enough, and brave enough, to figure out what was done and then find a way to reverse it. We're proud of you, sunshine."

Joy bubbled up, banishing her doubts and lifting her spirits. She lifted her head to smile up at him and found him staring down at her with a look that made her heart soar. "Thank you."

"All I did was tell you the truth." His voice dropped to a whisper. "And here's another truth. I love you."

"Even now you know who my father is?" she asked, already knowing the answer. Her men didn't care about things like that.

"Yes, even now I know about your family. I'm pretty sure we should never meet them, though. At least, not until your dad retires from office."

"Deal."

"Now that we've got that all figured out, shall we join the others? I believe Huey's got everything set up for a little combination celebration and welcome to the station party for Phaedra."

"How would Huey know about that?"

"Because we got word the second she arrived. We wanted to surprise you. Now, come on, you're holding up the festivities!" Blade called from the door.

"I don't think they heard you out in the waiting room. Next time yell a little louder." Lance muttered to his brother as he took Alyson's hand and led her out the door.

They bickered all the way to the elevator, and Alyson loved every moment. She was surrounded by her friends and lovers, all of them laughing and happy. For the first time in months, everyone was hopeful.

Their bubble of happiness burst the moment the doors to her private elevator opened. Sitting dead center in the middle of the floor was another elaborately folded piece of paper.

"Son of a starbeast," Dirk threw out an arm to stop anyone from getting too close.

"How did he get past the guards?"

"Could he still be here in the med-center?"

There was a flurry of questions, but she couldn't see who was saying what because Lance and Blade pulled her into the nearest corner and stepped in front of her.

Toro and Jaeger must have tried to do the same thing with Cynder because the next thing Alyson heard clearly was Cyn's angry refusal. "Not a chance, Dice man. You want to protect someone, stand in front of the cute little pink-haired human. If you try that protective crap on me again, I will kick your ass."

"Guys, it's a piece of paper. Don't you think you might be overreacting?" she asked, setting a hand on the pair of broad backs in front of her and pushing.

"No." Lance and Blade answered together.

From somewhere to her left, Phaedra snickered. "I like your friends already, Princess. Now, would someone explain why we're all staring at a piece of orange paper folded to look like a…is that a fox?"

"What the hell is a fox?" Dirk demanded.

"I need to take a look," Toro said.

There was something about his voice that caught Alyson's attention. Dirk must have heard it as well because she heard bodies jostling as if someone was moving aside.

"There. If it's like the last one, there will be a note written on it."

"Jaeg. You need to see this. Now." Toro sounded like he couldn't believe what he was seeing.

"*Fraxx*. It can't be," Jaeger said.

"It has to be."

"What the hell are you two talking about?" Blade demanded.

"We know someone who used to fold paper into shapes like this. Intricate designs like animals and figures."

"What about pyramids?" Alyson asked, projecting her voice to be heard.

"Yeah. He did those, too. But the fox was special to him. He had figures for all of us. Good luck totems, I guess you could call them."

"You served with him?" Dirk asked.

"He was our batch brother. Our leader, well, one of 'em. They were cloned commanders, like Luke and Kit. Vic was the one who picked up the paper folding habit though. We have no idea where he learned it," Toro said.

"And you think he's the one leaving these folded messages?" Blade asked, his voice tight.

"Someone you trusted and fought beside is threatening Alyson?"

"I don't know. It looks that way. Vic and Ward were good men. We lost touch with each other after the war. The last we heard, they were headed to the Drift." Jaeger's words were heavy with regret. "We should have looked harder for them."

Tired of not being able to see, Alyson finally pushed and prodded until Lance moved enough to let her pass him, though both he and Blade caught her hands before she went more than a few steps.

"That's close enough, sunshine."

"What does the note say? There is a note, right?" she asked.

The silence told her everything she needed to know. They hadn't touched anything yet. "Someone pick up the damned fox and check the elevator. I want to know what it says, and we should probably continue this conversation upstairs."

* * * *

Blade didn't leave Alyson's side until his brothers finished their sweep of her home and checked the security footage of the elevator to confirm that no one had used it to enter the residential area. The shielded figure showed up, but all he did was leave the note and leave.

By the time everything was confirmed secure, Alyson was pacing the entranceway in frustration.

She wanted to know more about the piece of paper, what might be written inside, and everything Toro and Jaeger could tell her about the man they thought might have left it for her.

The brothers were clearly disturbed by the thought that their batch siblings were involved in the threats against Alyson. Blade couldn't imagine how he'd feel if he were in their shoes.

"So, you think it's Victor leaving me these notes because of the way they're folded?"

Toro gave a half shrug. "How many people do you know would leave a message folded into the shape of a fox? Whatever is written on there is for you, but the animal is a message for Jaeger and me."

Jaeger nodded. "He and his brother had nicknames for us all. I was Hunter because that's what my name means in some old Earth dialect." He jerked a thumb at Toro. "He was Bull, for the same reason. They called themselves Fox and Wolf."

"I want to see what's written inside."

Dirk had donned a pair of hastily acquired surgical gloves before picking up the figure, ensuring he didn't disturb any fingerprints or trace evidence left behind. He kept the gloves on as he methodically unfolded the paper. The room went silent and still as everyone watched in anticipation.

There was a message inside, and by the time Dirk finished reading it aloud, Blade was already running through scenarios, working out the best way to keep Alyson alive.

The note was brief.

"Well Done. Now Run. I've held him off as long as I can. The Reaper is coming."

"Who the *fraxx* is the Reaper?" Phaedra asked.

"An assassin. A very good one. If Vic says run, then you should go. Now," Jaeger said, looking straight at Alyson.

"I can't go anywhere. I have work to finish here. Nya's next to get the cure. The next batch has to be set up…"

"Wrong answer, Doc. You did what you had to do, now it's time to let someone else take over," Blade said.

"But—"

"No buts. No arguments. You promised that when the time came, you'd do as we asked. Now is that time." Dirk pointed toward Alyson's room. "Go with Blade. Pack one small bag. Be back here in five minutes."

"I still don't like it when you boss me around," she complained but did as he said.

"Noted. Now, move your ass."

Blade followed her as she said a quick goodbye to everyone and made the short walk to her room. He expected her to try arguing again once they were behind closed doors, but she didn't say a word. Instead, she went to her closet and pulled out a battered looking carryall.

"I'm not even going to ask if you're okay. So, how about this question instead. What can I do to help you right now?"

Alyson set the bag on the bed and went straight back to her closet to rifle through her clothes. "You could tell me what you and your brothers are saying to each other right now. I know you're talking to them via your internal link. What's the plan? Dirk told me to pack, but I have no idea what I should bring. Where are we going? For how long?"

There was no time for gentle words, so Blade gave her the unvarnished truth. She was strong enough to handle it. "We don't have a destination, yet. And we'll be gone as long as it takes to neutralize the Reaper and make sure you're safe. Dirk's arranging for transport, and Lance is packing for the three of us."

She continued pulling clothes out of the closet and tossing them on the bed. Her face was turned away from him, but her back was rigid, and her shoulders were stiff with tension.

"How are Jaeger and Toro taking the news?"

"About as well as could be expected. They're headed back to the Nova with Cynder and Phaedra, and they've made it known they want to be part of any attempt to apprehend their batch brother."

"I can't blame them for that." Alyson finished with her closet and moved on to a chest of drawers, rapidly opening each one and taking out a few things. The stack on the bed was growing quickly, but they were short on time.

"You're going to need shoes." He reminded her.

She finally turned to face him, giving him a wry smile. "Right. Thanks."

"Can I start putting this in the bag for you?" He pointed to the stack of clothing.

"Roll it up and stuff in whatever will fit. I have no idea what I'm going to need, so I'm taking a bit of everything."

She froze. "I'm going to need my medical bag, too. It's in my office. I can't leave it behind."

"You won't need—"

"We can't be sure what I'll need, and I'd feel naked without it."

"I'll tell Dirk to grab it." He probably should have stopped there, but he couldn't resist adding. "We can't have you feeling naked. Not until we get you safely away from here and can make that happen for real."

They finished packing with thirty seconds to spare. Lance and Dirk were already there, armed and ready to take on the galaxy. His weapons and go bag were already waiting for him, and he geared up while Dirk and Lance showed Alyson how to put on the simple body armor shirt they had liberated from Corp-Sec's inventory in the event things went sideways. He could hear them giving her a quick rundown on what would happen next. The three of them had worked out a variety of plans days ago, hoping like hell they would never need to initiate any of them.

So much for hope.

Now the goal was to get to Zura's old ship, the *Sun Sprite*, and get as far as they could from the cold-blooded killer who had the women they loved in his crosshairs.

CHAPTER THIRTEEN

Alyson wanted to explain things to Anne before she left, but that plan was shot down the instant she brought it up. While she had been packing Dirk and Lance had put an elaborate plan in motion, one that didn't allow time for anything as sentimental as saying goodbye to friends, or even telling her employees that she was leaving.

"But the med-center. I need to explain to Anne..."

"Zale is going to talk to her after we're gone. He's got the passcodes to the lab and your office and instructions to bring one of the other doctors up to speed. You can give the name to Anne once we're underway."

"What about Phaedra and the data she brought?"

"Mack and Dash are handling the data. Phaedra will be safe in the Nova Club, and you need to stop asking questions. Our transport will be here in two minutes. It's time to go." Dirk jerked his head toward the elevator. "Once you're in, you stay there until we tell you to step out. Blade, you take point."

"Got it." Blade lifted her bag and set it on her shoulder. "Keep your head down, eyes open, and no matter what, you have to keep up." He cupped her cheek in one hand and winked at her. "We'll have you safe, sound, and naked before you know it."

Lance snorted. "That's a hell of a pep talk."

"Not the time," Dirk snapped.

They crowded into the elevator, and the moment the doors opened on the main level, Blade was out the door, one hand brushing the firearm holstered at his hip. Dirk and Blade grabbed her by the arms, half-lifting her off the floor as they took off after their brother at a dead run.

There wasn't time for her to answer any of the surprised questions and calls of her staff and patients as they rushed her past the exam rooms, through the waiting room, and out into the space station's main promenade.

There was an armored Corp-Sec transport waiting for them, along with a number of armed Corp-Sec officers who stood shoulder to shoulder to form a secure cordon from the main doors to the vehicle.

"Head down," Lance reminded her, and then they were moving again.

Once they were all inside, the transport took off immediately with Blade in the driver's seat. He executed a near-vertical takeoff, taking the vehicle high over the crowded causeway before accelerating so hard she was pushed down into her seat. She expected the tension to ease now they were underway, but that didn't happen. No one spoke, and everyone was grim-faced and on edge.

"I take it that we're not in the clear, yet?"

Blade couldn't turn around to look at her directly, but he managed to glance backward at her for a moment and flashed her a ghost of a smile. "Not yet, no. While there are plenty of ships we could get passage on, the Reaper has to know we're more likely to use one of Zura's. Since the *Sun Sprite* is the only one currently docked, it won't take him long to figure out where we're going. He wasn't waiting for you outside the med center, so the odds are good that if he's going to make an attempt on your life, he'll do it when we try to get aboard the *Sprite*."

"If he knows that's where we're going, why aren't we taking another ship?"

Lance answered her next question. "Because we can trust Royan and Owen. Royan's our pilot, and Owen Connor's a security guard at the Nova. They were prepping to leave on a run anyway, so they're already onboard and ready to take off as soon as we get there. If we booked passage on another ship, we wouldn't know who to trust. This is safer," Blade explained.

"None of this makes any sense. Why is the Reaper after me? I thought he worked for the cartels, not the corporations. How would the corporations even be able to hire him?"

Dirk took over the conversation and Lance went back to staring out the window, looking for threats she knew they couldn't possibly see. Not traveling this fast.

"There's obviously some connection between this Victor guy and the Reaper. Hopefully, he'll be able to give us some answers once we find him."

Alyson knew she was asking a lot of questions, but she needed to understand what was happening. She was trying to diagnose this whole situation, and she didn't have enough information, yet. "How do we find Victor? And who is looking for him? Corp-Sec? Our friends?"

"Both. Jaeger sent images of Victor and Ward to Corp-Sec. They're currently scanning the entire station for a facial recognition hit. When there's a hit, a team will move in, and likely Jaeger and Toro will be with them."

"What if we didn't leave? If we never showed up at the *Sun Sprite*, he would have no idea where I was, right?" Maybe she could talk them into letting her stay on the station. If she was here, she could still help somehow. Anything would be better than running away to leave her friends to face this threat alone.

"We're getting you off this station, Aly. End of conversation," Dirk said.

Lance wrapped an arm around her shoulders and pulled her into his side. "We can't protect you here. Vic's last note made that clear. We need to get you somewhere where we have more control. Now that we know who is after you, we can make a plan and end this."

"It doesn't feel right to leave when everyone else is staying here. They're going to be taking all the chances while I'm flying away."

The car was silent for a moment and then Lance exhaled slowly and turned toward her. "They won't be in nearly as much danger once you're gone. They'll close the med-center for a few days and secure it as best they can while they produce as much of that cure as possible. The instructions on how to synthesize it will go out soon, and then there will be no stopping the news from spreading. You won your battle, sunshine. If you're not here, everyone will be safer. You're the Reaper's target, and what little information Corp-Sec has on this guy indicates he doesn't stop until his target is terminated or he's called off by whoever controls him."

It made sense. The best thing she could do for her friends was to draw the danger away from them. It still wasn't easy to accept, though.

"We're going to keep you safe. No matter what it takes, you are going to live to see the changes you've started," Dirk said.

"Stop saying that." She pulled out of Lance's embrace as another thought hit her. "What if I went, but you stayed? You could go back to work for Corp-Sec and help track down the Reaper. Or stay at my place and guard the medical center. Then maybe it could stay open? You're abandoning your jobs and your friends to protect me, but if you're right, once I'm on the ship I should be safe enough. There's no reason you have to come with me."

All three of them started talking at once.

"Like hell we're not going with you."

"What do you mean, there's no reason we have to come?"

"You need us."

"You don't need to do this," she said when they finally let her back into the conversation. "This is too dangerous. I can't ask this of you."

"Of course it's dangerous. If it wasn't we'd all be relaxing somewhere right now, preferably naked. That's the *fraxxing* point, Doc," Blade retorted.

She shook her head. After a lifetime of standing alone, she finally had someone on her side, fighting with her, and she was terrified of losing them because they'd chosen to stand by her. "You'd be safer if you stayed."

"We love you. That's the only reason we need to come with you and make sure you're safe. The day you started working on a way to reverse cyborg infertility, you made a choice. You knew the risks you were taking, but you did it anyway. This is *our* choice," Lance said.

Her heart soared even as fear gripped her with steely claws. So much was at stake.

"We are not your parents. We're not going to let you walk out of our lives. You're not alone anymore. You've got us." Dirk hauled her into his lap and locked his arms around her as he if expected her to jump out of the transport mid-flight.

"I can't lose you. It would be easier to let you go now than to watch you get hurt because of me."

"No one's letting anyone go. Not now. Not ever," Blade stated.

"Never?" she asked.

"Never," Dirk whispered.

"Promise me."

"We promise. We love you, Alyson."

All three of them spoke with one voice, and it made her heart overflow with joy and a dozen other wondrous emotions she couldn't put a name to. They were the words she'd been waiting to hear for her entire life, and she'd found them at the far end of the galaxy, surrounded by danger, and protected by three of the bravest, most incredible men she'd ever known.

"I love you, too. That's why I want you to stay here. You're safer that way. If something happened to one of you while you were protecting me…" she trailed off, unable to finish her sentence. The thought hurt too much to put into words.

"Now?" Blade said from the front. "You had to tell us you love us now, while I'm driving and can't claim a celebratory kiss?"

Lance chuckled. "Your timing is as bad as Dirk's. I'm still happy as hell to hear you say it, though."

Dirk nuzzled her hair, and when he spoke, his voice was a husky murmur by her ear. "When you love someone, you'd do anything to keep them safe. The reason you want us to stay here is the same reason we need to come with you."

"Promise me none of you are going to do anything stupid, like sacrificing yourselves to protect me."

Silence filled the cab.

"You're all stubborn as hell and more than a little insane. You know that, right?" she asked when it was clear none of them were going to agree to her terms.

"We know. We're also the best chance you have of enjoying a long, healthy life. Since we're hoping to be part of that life, we've got a vested interest in keeping you alive," Lance said.

There wasn't any point in pressing them for a promise none of them would give her, so she didn't try. If luck was with them, then they would escape without anyone needing to risk anything.

*

Even before the transport stopped moving, Lance had a feeling their next step wasn't going to be easy. The hairs on the back of his neck were standing on end. Someone was watching them. Waiting out of sight.

"He's here," Dirk said via their internal channel.

"Yeah. I feel it, too. But where's he hiding?" he sent back.

"He's here, isn't he?" Alyson asked.

"We think so." Dirk kissed her hard and then set her back down on the seat.

In less than two minutes they'd be on the ground again, and they'd be on their own. The Corp-Sec officers that had protected them at the medical center were on their way, but it would take them a few minutes to get loaded into the transports and catch up. That's time Alyson didn't have. They'd have to run this gauntlet on their own. Well, not quite. They did have someone else they could call in.

Blade hit a button on the dashboard, and Royan's face appeared on the vid-screen a few seconds later. "Engines are heating, and the beer is on ice. When's the party starting?"

"We're three minutes out, but we think we've got a gate crasher."

Royan didn't seem concerned at all. In fact, he looked thrilled. "Does this mean I get to shoot someone? Do you have any idea how long it's been since I got into a decent fight?"

"You're a lunatic. I like that about you. We're going to need you and Owen to cover us until we make it to the outer docking arm. Wherever this bastard is lying in wait, he won't be in the ring itself. There's no place to hide in there, it's nothing but hallway."

"He could be waiting on one of the other ships berthed nearby." Royan pointed out.

"There are no other ships in that area. Your sister called in some favors and had them all moved."

Royan laughed. "You mean she threatened to cut off someone's tab at the Nova if they didn't make things happen. I know how she operates. Right. Owen's already on his way to you, and I'm leaving now. See you soon."

"I'm glad he and his sister are on our side," Blade muttered as he deactivated the vid-link.

"You and me both," Alyson said.

Lance touched her hand to get her attention. "We're going to be landing in a few seconds. Same drill as before. You stay between us, with your head down and keep your cute ass moving. If we tell you to run, you will do as we say and sprint for the ship. One of us will be with you every step of the way."

Tight-lipped and frowning, Alyson nodded in understanding. If they issued the order, she'd go, but he knew damned well she didn't like the idea of leaving any of them behind. He didn't like the idea of leaving her, either, but if things went sideways, they'd operate better knowing she was out of the line of fire.

Dirk was out the door the moment they touched down, and Alyson was right behind him. Lance followed up as fast as he could, moving in close to screen her from view. Blade came around the vehicle and jogged past them to take point. The second he was in position, they moved forward together, causing no small amount of panic and outcry as they ran, openly armed, past several clusters of off-duty crewmen and station personnel.

He could feel eyes on them. The bastard was watching. But where was he? In the crowd? Perched somewhere overhead? Lance wished his instincts would give him something more concrete to go on than a scrotum-tightening sense of imminent danger.

He got his answer before they made it thirty feet. Something slammed into the center of his back. His body armor took the brunt of the damage, but the strike still packed enough force to make him misstep and stagger. A gap opened between himself and Alyson. She was vulnerable.

"I'm hit. Go!" Even as he bellowed the words, the first wave of pain washed over him. He deactivated his pain receptors and charged after the others.

Dirk reached back and grabbed Alyson, pulling her forward with enough force that her feet left the ground. It's a good thing he did, too, because a split-second later a laser bolt sliced through the air where she had been. The bastard was good. He had deliberately targeted Lance to slow him down enough to get a shot at his main target.

The air around them filled with bolts of sizzling light, some of them coming from a point ahead of them. Royan and Owen had joined the fight, shifting the odds back to their favor.

The Reaper didn't appreciate their involvement. He switched targets and started slamming the source of their cover fire with a barrage of shots that made Lance wince. The station's superstructure was impressive, but it was far from new. If it took too much damage, it would fail. This close to the outer hull, any kind of failure would mean an atmospheric breach.

"Is he *fraxxing* insane?" Alyson asked aloud, though she didn't seem to realize she'd said anything at all.

"Save your breath for running," Lance reminded her.

She risked a brief glance over her shoulder and gave him a wide-eyed nod, then put on an extra burst of adrenaline-fuelled speed to catch up with Dirk.

By the time they reached cover, the walls around them were pitted and glowing red-hot in places, but they looked to be in better shape than Royan did. He was lying a few feet away from Owen, who was still laying down covering fire in an attempt to keep their adversary trapped in place. Dirk drew his blaster and knelt next to Owen, adding his firepower to the attempt.

"Your sister is going to kill you when she finds out you let yourself get shot," Alyson muttered as she dropped to her knees beside Royan.

He'd been shot in the shoulder, leaving a charred, bloody wound that had to hurt like hell.

Royan uttered a wheezing laugh and shook his head. "Naw, she's used to seeing me bleeding. You need to go, Doc." He rolled his head toward the corridor that stretched out behind him.

"I'm not leaving you lying here, wounded."

"Yeah, you are." Blade grabbed hold of the back of her body armor and lifted her off the deck. "Head for the ship. Now."

"But—"

"Medi-bots." Royan tapped his chest weakly. "I'll be fine."

"You'd better be." She turned and ran with Blade only a half-stride behind her.

"You're in no shape to pilot anything but a bed in medical," Lance said.

"One of you will have to do it. You can fly a ship, right? Please tell me that's somewhere in your programming. And for *fraxx* sakes, don't let anything happen to your woman or that ship, or Zura will cut us into pieces and toss them out an airlock one chunk at a time."

"Dirk's a decent pilot. All I need are the security codes. I don't imagine your ship's AI is going to let us fly away without them. Don't worry, we'll bring back everyone, and everything, in one piece."

Twenty seconds later, Lance had all the information he needed. "Time to go."

Dirk got to his feet. "We owe you both. Thanks."

Royan managed another weak grin. "I should be thanking you. A firefight, a new scar to add to the collection, and if I'm lucky, Owen will come see me in medical and kiss all my boo-boos better."

"Dream on," Owen called over his shoulder.

"Dreaming about you is my favorite pastime, baby."

Owen shook his head. "And here I was worried you were seriously hurt. If you can flirt, you're clearly going to be fine. You had me worried, idiot."

Royan closed his eyes and smiled. "He was worried about me. I'm making progress."

A cacophony of approaching sirens announced the arrival of Corp-Sec. The hunt for the Reaper was about to start in earnest, which meant they were out of danger, for now.

"Thanks for the help. Tell Zura we'll take good care of her ship," Lance joined Dirk, and the two of them hurried to the *Sprite's* berth.

Blade and Alyson were waiting for them a few feet beyond the door.

"Mind your head." Blade pointed to the pipes and conduits that ran along the ceiling of the cramped corridor.

"What's going on out there? Who's going to pilot the ship? Are we staying here?" Alyson's questions came tumbling out in a single breath.

"Bring her up to speed while I get us out of here. Lance, I'll need those codes." Dirk was already squeezing past the others on his way to the cockpit.

Space was going to be an issue for the next while. The *Sprite* was a working vessel designed for speed and power, not comfort. She'd had a full refit less than a year ago, and already there were already dents in the deck plating and other signs of constant use.

Lance sent Dirk everything he needed in a quick data burst via their internal link. Dirk acknowledged it with a wave of his hand before stepping through a bulkhead door and vanishing from sight.

"I can give you a sit-rep while we hunt down the crew quarters. Any guesses on where those would be?" Lance turned to look down the corridor that stretched the length of the ship.

"Lance, you're hurt!"

Alyson's agitated exclamation confused him for a moment. In all the excitement of the last few minutes, he'd forgotten about the hit he'd taken at the beginning of the attack. The pain block was still holding, so he couldn't feel a thing.

"It's nothing," he said absently, still trying to figure out the most likely place to find their quarters.

"It doesn't look like nothing. Your jacket's destroyed and the armor below is melted to slag. How are you even functioning right now?"

"My implants. A soldier too injured to fight was of no value to our masters or the war effort, remember? We can block pain at will. Whatever it takes to stay on our feet until the mission ends."

Alyson moved to his side, her lips pursed and her eyes dark with worry. "Then consider the mission ended. I want to see you in whatever passes for a med-bay on this ship right away. You can give me the rep-sit, or whatever you called it, on the way there. Ship? Give me the location of the med-bay, please."

"The med-bay is located aft of your position, on the main deck." A woman's voice informed them, her tone surprisingly sultry for a computer program.

"Go." She pointed in the direction the ship had stated.

"Yes, ma'am." He managed to hide his grin until he was facing the empty corridor. After what she'd been through, plenty of people would be losing their minds, but not Alyson. She was already back to her usual self; issuing orders and putting everyone else's needs ahead of her own.

CHAPTER FOURTEEN

Alyson hadn't even finished checking Lance's burns when the ship's standard engines rumbled to life. Even though he didn't really need it, she took the time to apply a coat of healing accelerating ointment to his injuries. Not that there was much for her to treat. The body armor had done its job and absorbed most of the heat and damage, and the medi-bots had already started healing what little damage there was.

Still, she did what she could to speed up the healing process. Being in a med-bay, surrounded by the familiar scent of ointment and antiseptics as the medical scanners beeped and hummed helped her reclaim her sense of normalcy after what had been a far from normal day.

Throughout her examination, Lance had filled her in on the details she'd been too busy running for her life to really register. Even now, most of it was a blur, with only a few details standing out here and there. The sizzle of laser fire. The nose-tingling scent of ozone that had filled the air at the height of the shooting, the heart-clenching sense of vulnerability that filled her as they'd made the run to cover.

"You're amazing." Lance's words startled her out of her recollections.

"What? No. I'm really not."

He rose from the bed where he'd been sitting while she treated him and folded her into his arms. "Yeah, you are. One day, you're going to learn to stop arguing with us about everything."

"I don't see that happening." She started to wrap her arms around his waist, then remembered his back was covered in ointment and settled for resting her hands on his hips. She could feel his chuckle even before she could hear it, a low thrum of amusement that rolled up from deep in his chest.

"To be honest, neither do I. You're as stubborn as we are, which is probably a good thing."

He cradled her close, and the tension that gripped her started to ease. When one of them held her, it was as if the world and all its danger faded into the background for a little while. She was a believer in science, not magic, but there was something a little mystical about the way they made her feel with even a simple touch. Protected. Empowered. Cherished.

They stayed that way until she felt the telltale drop and sway of the ship uncoupling from its docking anchors and moving out into space. They were on their way; which meant they needed to rejoin the others and figure out where in the universe they were actually *going*.

When she started to move away, Lance murmured a wordless protest and dipped his head to kiss her. Her stomach did another drop, and this one had nothing to do with the ship. His lips moved across hers, and when she kissed him back he groaned, crushing her against him so tightly she could feel his heart beating.

The tip of his tongue swept across her lips, and she parted them, letting him in. There were a thousand things she should be thinking about right now, but she pushed them all out of her head. She'd survived an attack on her life. If that wasn't grounds for a little celebrating, she didn't know what was.

She moaned and rose up on her toes as his tongue danced with hers. His hands were everywhere, stroking and teasing as he made love to her mouth with a hunger that left her weak-kneed. Their bodies rubbed together, building up a delicious friction that threatened to ignite into a firestorm of raw need.

"Are you two going to join us anytime soon, or should we go ahead and make plans without you?" Blade's voice sounded over the ship's PA system.

"I'm tempted to tell them to go ahead without us," Lance muttered.

"Me too, but I know what will happen if I do. Blade and Dirk will decide I need to be locked in a bunker somewhere until the danger is passed, and I won't be there insisting that whatever happens next, I'm going to be part of it."

"Stubborn woman."

She stuck out her tongue at him and laughed. "And you love me for it."

* * * *

Since they had yet to decide on a destination, Dirk opted to stick to the heavily traveled routes leading away from the Drift. Heading deeper into the system meant navigating the massive field of asteroids that were all that was left of what had once been two of the system's planets, so he pointed the ship toward civilized space. Once they'd decided where they were going, he'd plot a course and activate the FTL drive.

All four of them couldn't fit into the cockpit of the *Sun Sprite*, so he and Alyson were in the pilots' seats while Lance and Blade were crammed into the doorway. At Alyson's request, he had activated the rear viewscreen. The four of them had spent the last hour sitting in silence, watching as the winking lights of Astek Station and the rest of the Drift were slowly lost to view.

"Do you think he's coming after us?" Alyson asked, her eyes still on the viewscreen despite the fact there was nothing to see but a near infinite field of black space and cold starlight.

"I think that, until we hear otherwise, we have to assume that the Reaper is still a threat." Dirk had hoped that they would get news that the Reaper had been caught by now and he could turn the ship around and head back. It wasn't likely to happen, but that hadn't stopped him from hoping, anyway.

Alyson sighed and massaged the back of her neck before swinging her chair around to face the others. "So, where do we go? I'd suggest heading to Cassien Alpha, but I'm sure the bastard hunting me knows enough about my family and former friends to find me anywhere I could hide on that planet."

"It's the first place he'd look for you," Blade agreed.

"We've got a fully fuelled and stocked ship and a whole galaxy to choose from. The only thing we don't have is a whole lot of scrip, so we're not going to any exclusive resort planets," Lance said.

"Who said we don't have scrip?" Alyson asked.

She had a gleam in her eye that reminded Dirk of his brothers when they were up to something.

"Is there something you'd like to share with us, Aly?" Dirk prompted.

"You can't access your regular accounts. There's every chance the Reaper will be watching them," Blade reminded her.

"I don't need to access my regular accounts. Back when I was still roommates with Phaedra, she helped me set up an account with a highly secure, off-world bank. The kind no one can hack. Not even her. She wanted to be sure Bryce couldn't get his greedy paws on my inheritance. She never trusted him."

"Inheritance?" Blade leaned into the cockpit and waggled his brows. "Oh, baby. Tell me you're rich, and I'll propose right here and now."

"Maybe you should save the proposals until after we've defeated the assassin and disseminated the cure for cyborg infertility." She blinked and burst out laughing. "Wow. When did my life become the plot of a bad movie?"

"It's not a bad movie, it's a blockbuster! Action. Adventure, and not one, not two, but three incredibly sexy leading men," Blade said. "And you're changing the subject again. What inheritance?"

She shrugged. "I'm not obscenely wealthy or anything, but when my paternal grandmother died, she left my brother and me sizeable trust funds. If we need scrip, I've got access to plenty of it."

"And that explains how you can afford to run the med-center the way you do." Lance gave her a knowing look.

She scowled and folded her arms across her chest. "What's wrong with the way I run my business?"

"For one thing, sunshine, you only charge your patients what they can afford, and some of them can't afford the cost of a bandage, never mind a full course of healing accelerants."

"Or surgery," Blade added.

"And I've never seen you turn away anyone. Not once. You've got a generous heart, and a kind soul, but as far as business plans go, that's really no way to make any money."

"Oh, that. I donate most of my salary back into the medical center to offset those costs."

All three of them stared at her, dumbstruck.

"What?"

You donate your salary?" Lance asked.

"Not all of it." She shrugged. "It's only money. I have more than I need, so I share it with those who don't have enough. It's what my grandparents did when they ran their own practice. I wanted to be like them. I even took their last name when I graduated. I'm a Jefferies, like them. The Caldwell way of life didn't really suit me."

"One day, I hope we get to meet your grandparents." Dirk wanted to thank them for encouraging Alyson and helping her become the incredible woman he loved.

"I'd like to meet them, too. I mean, if you think they can deal with the idea of you being with three cyborgs." Lance said.

Fraxx. With everything that had happened, Dirk hadn't had time to process who Alyson's family was, and what that might mean. Out on the Drift, things were different, but it wasn't uncommon for powerful, influential families like Alyson's to still have some outdated and unforgiving attitudes when it came to relationships.

"You'd really want to meet them?" Alyson was smiling, and her expression eased the tightness that had started to grip his heart. "When this is all over, I can arrange a trip home. It's been too long since I saw them last, and I know they'd like very much to meet the men I'm dating. It won't bother them at all that you're cyborgs, or that I'm dating more than one man at a time. If I'm happy, they'll be happy for me. "

"When this is over, we'll go to Cassien Alpha and meet them." Dirk said.

Alyson uttered a wistful sigh. "Home cooking, fresh air, and long walks in the woods. Are you sure we can't go there right now?"

"Soon." They all said at once.

The trouble was, they had no idea if it was true or not.

A steady chirping noise started coming from the console in front of him, and Dirk started looking for the source. The console's layout was newer than anything he'd worked with before, but the basic layout wasn't all that different from the mining ship where he'd gotten his first hands-on training as a pilot.

There was an incoming vid message, and it was tagged with Mack's Corp-Sec ID. Anticipation had everyone leaning in to listen as he activated the vid-screen and Mack's face appeared, his grim expression making it clear that he didn't have good news to share.

"What happened? Is everyone okay?" Alyson asked.

"Two Corp-Sec officers are in surgery right now, but they're both expected to make it. The suspect was shielded, which was how he got the drop on them. Everyone else is fine, including Royan. He's in the med-center, too, but he's healing so quickly they expect him to be discharged in the morning."

Alyson exhaled in relief. "I'm glad to hear that. I guess that means the only one still in serious trouble is me, huh?"

"It looks that way. We've got teams sweeping the station and computers running facial recognition programs and reviewing every scrap of surveillance footage, but so far we're coming up empty. If the bastard is still on board the station, we have to assume he won't be for long."

Alyson started asking for more information about the medical status of the injured, but before she got her answer, Dirk was distracted by Dash's voice inside his head.

"While Mack's performing for whoever might be listening, I'm going to give you a quick rundown on what else is going on."

"I'm listening."

"It took Alyson's friend Phaedra about twenty damned minutes to work some sort of computer wizardry and track down where the Reaper was hiding out. Toro and Jaeger went in with a team, and they found their brother, Victor. He's in bad shape, but he managed to confirm a few things. He and his clone are

both the Reaper. Two men, one face. One kills, one establishes an alibi by being seen far from the crime."

"What happened to Victor? Will he recover?"

Dash didn't answer for a second, and when he did, his words were tangled with emotions so strong they traveled across their shared link. *"The medics think he'll recover. At least, his physical wounds should heal. Mental and emotional wounds are another issue. They've been reprogrammed, Dirk. The fraxxing corporation who took them reactivated their obedience subroutines and enhanced them for good measure."*

"They were taken? By who? How?" The ramifications of what Dash was saying made it hard for Dirk to focus. Taken. Obedience. Reprogramming. The words bounced around inside his head while his stomach twisted itself into knots. This was the stuff of every cyborg's nightmares.

"The only one who can tell us that is Victor, and he's unconscious right now. When we know more, we'll let you know. This comm link won't work once you get too far away, but Phaedra is working on setting up some encryption so we can keep in contact. I'll send the decryption key in a data burst in a minute. There will be some coordinates in the burst, too. They'll bring you to an automated resupply station Phaedra knows of. She says it's been abandoned for years. There's no fuel or supplies there, but it's still got a breathable atmosphere and an active AI. I don't want to know how she knows that. She's broken more privacy and anti-hacking laws

in the short time she's been sitting in our office than I can count."

"The resupply station sounds like our best chance at finding a defensible position. Thanks." Dirk paused, then added, *"If Toro or Jaeger think of anything that might help us understand the way their brother thinks, we could use the intel. I don't want to have to kill him…"*

"If it comes to a choice between him or Alyson, you do what you have to. Once we have more actionable intel, we'll share it with Zale's friend in the IAF. This is too big for us to handle on our own. It's time for the military to get involved."

"Agreed." The IAF had an entire division dedicated to policing the corporations and ensuring they didn't break planetary or galactic law. If they weren't aware of what the hell the corporations were doing, it was past time that they found out.

Tell the others good luck from me, and we'll see you all when this is over," Dash said.

"Stay safe."

Mack was saying his goodbyes to the others when Dirk tuned back into the conversation going on around him. He added his farewells to the rest and terminated the call.

"We've got a possible destination, and I've got news you're all going to want to hear."

Alyson spun around in her chair so fast her hair whipped into her face, momentarily blinding her. "What news? What destination? How?"

She swiped at her hair in annoyance, leaned forward, and did a fair impression of his tone when she demanded, "Explain. Now."

"It's a little terrifying how well you do that, Doc," Blade said with a snicker.

"I learned from the best," she retorted before narrowing her eyes at Dirk. "Who were you talking to while I was chatting with Mack? Because we were clearly having different conversations."

"Dash." He tapped his temple. "It was important no one intercepted the message he had for me. Well, for us."

"What did Dash have to say that was so important?"

He explained about the deactivated resupply station first, and by the time he was done with his explanation, the data burst Dash had promised arrived.

"I've got the coordinates now. Does anyone have another destination for us to consider, or do we trust Phaedra and go to this station?"

"There are only a handful of people I'd trust my life with. Three of them are here with me, and Phaedra's one of the others. If she thinks that's the best place for us to make our stand, then I say we go."

"No bystanders to worry about, no potential allies in place already, and we'll have the advantage of getting there first," Lance said.

"If we're going up against a known killer, we're going to need every advantage we can get. Especially if this guy turns out to be a cyborg."

Dirk cleared his throat. "And that brings me to my other news."

He caught them up on everything Dash had shared, ending with the gut-twisting facts about what had been done to both Victor and Ward. When he was done, the cockpit was silent.

"But we're protected..." Lance started to say, then trailed off.

Blade slammed his hand into the bulkhead. "We're *supposed* to be protected. Free citizens of the galaxy and all that. But we've always known the corporations don't all agree with that assessment. They built us, and they still think of us as their property. We're commodities, not people."

"They were taken, and then reprogrammed?" Alyson was pale and visibly shaken by what she'd learned. "And now one of them has been ordered to kill me."

"That's not going to happen." It didn't matter if there was an army of cyborg assassins coming after Alyson, they'd find a way to keep her safe. She was their light in a dark and unforgiving universe. After years spent drifting, they had finally found their purpose. Her.

"It's decided then." Dirk programmed in the coordinates and prepped the FTL engines. Even at faster-than-light speed, it would take more than a week to arrive at their destination, especially since he wasn't programming it as one long jump, but a series of shorter ones. That should stop the Reaper—Ward—from being able to figure out where they were headed until he tracked them to their final jump point.

There wasn't any doubt in Dirk's mind that the assassin would follow them. Ward's behavioral programming wouldn't let him do anything else. He had to finish his mission, and they had to stop him.

* * * *

Once they were in transit, Dirk activated the AI's autopilot, and they went to find something to eat. They talked about what they knew and speculated on what they didn't as they explored the menu of the ship's food dispenser. It wasn't the way any of them had hoped to celebrate Alyson's accomplishment. Instead of a party with her friends at the Nova, it was the four of them, some mediocre cupcakes from the dispenser, and a keg of Torskian ale Blade found stashed in the galley.

"This stuff isn't getting any easier to drink." Alyson set down her mostly empty glass of ale hard enough to make every other glass on the table jump.

"That's because it's got more in common with engine degreaser than anything you should be drinking. Is this stuff actually safe for human consumption?" Lance asked.

"It hasn't killed Royan, yet. So, I'd say so."

"I'm not convinced Royan's actually human. I've seen him drink enough to put a Torski under the table." Blade moved the glass out of Alyson's reach before she could take another drink.

"I do not need you three protecting me from a glass of alien hooch."

"That's debatable." For the second time in a day, Dirk indulged himself by scooping Alyson out of her seat and into his lap.

She settled in with a contented sigh that made his heart turn to taffy.

"This is getting to be a habit."

Blade chuckled. "Haven't you noticed? When Dirk's feeling grumpy, you wind up in his arms or his lap. You're his living, breathing teddy bear. It's really adorable."

"I do not need a teddy bear. I'm not the childish one in this family." Dirk tucked Alyson's head under his chin and let the comforting warmth of her body soak into his skin. She wasn't his teddy bear, she was the center of his universe, and the only woman who had ever made him feel at peace.

"If I'm your teddy bear, then you're my squishy," Alyson declared.

Oh, hell no. Both his brothers burst out laughing, and his doom was sealed.

I'm not your squishy."

"Are too."

Lance was laughing so hard he was tearing up, and Blade was about to slide under the table, the traitorous bastards. So be it, if he was going down, they were going down with him. "Not that I'm agreeing to anything, but, if you think I should be your squishy, then what are you going to call those two idiots?"

The laughter stopped almost instantly.

"Pookie and snuggles." Alyson pointed to Blade, then Lance as she christened them.

Blade groaned in horror. "That's it. You're never allowed to drink Torskian ale again. Ever."

"I'm good with snuggles, actually. Every time you use that nickname, I'm going to take it as an invitation." Lance crooked his finger at Alyson. "Want to come over here and collect?"

Dirk let her go. She hopped to her feet, swayed, and grabbed at the table. "Woah."

"I've got you." Dirk had her back in his arms in seconds.

"And I'd say that means it's time tuck you in, sunshine." Lance glanced over at Blade. "Where the hell are we sleeping, anyway?"

"Wait until you see the captain's quarters. Zura must have had it redone when the ship went in for a refit because it will accommodate all of us very nicely."

Alyson giggled. "She wanted to be sure there was room for her and her husbands to sleep comfortably when they were on board. She had a hell of a time getting the designers to understand the changes until she flat out told them she was married to two big cyborgs who took up a lot of space in bed."

"Well, they must have listened, because it's the roomiest crew cabin I've ever seen," Blade said before leading them out of the galley.

"When this is over, I should talk to Zura, then. See who she used and if they can do something similar with my place."

"Whatever you want, love."

All three of them grinned. The future was looking better all the time. All they had to do was survive long enough to make it a reality.

CHAPTER FIFTEEN

If anyone had told Blade that some of the best days of his life would be spent on board a cargo freighter while on the run from an assassin, he would have asked for a sample of whatever pharma they were using. It was true, though. He'd enjoyed every minute of the past five days.

There were no threats to watch for, no reason to stay vigilant against potential danger. They could finally relax, and so could Alyson. There were no patients out here, no demands on her time, no reasons to push herself to the point of exhaustion. They were all enjoying a brief hiatus from reality, made all the sweeter because they knew it wouldn't last.

Over the past few days, Blade had started to realize that what he felt for Alyson hadn't been love, not when he'd first said the words. It had only been the promise of love, but with every hour that passed, that promise continued to evolve and grow into something greater. A week ago he would have died for her. Now, he wanted to live for her instead.

For that to work, Alyson needed to survive, too, and right now she wasn't listening to any of their suggestions on how to make sure that happened. She stubbornly insisted on being included instead of agreeing to hide on the *Sun Sprite* until the danger had passed.

They were sitting in the ship's rec area, and the afternoon's planning session was rapidly spinning out of control.

"No, damn it. We've talked about this. You're his target, so it makes no sense for you to be out in the open," Lance argued.

"I won't be out in the open. According to the blueprints Phaedra managed to find, there are two easily defendable locations on the station." Alyson stabbed a finger into the hologram that filled the air over their heads. "Here and here."

"Which is why you should be way the hell over here." Lance pointed to a docking arm on the far side of the station.

"And what happens if he comes after me on the ship? You'll be too far away to stop him. As much as I've enjoyed the self-defence lessons you guys have given me over the last few days, but I'm hardly ready to take on a trained killer single-handed."

"The *Sprite's* AI is capable of defending this ship for a prolonged period. You'll be safer here." Dirk's voice was tight with barely checked frustration.

They all wanted her to be as safe as they could possibly make her, and none of them wanted her to witness the fight that was coming.

Blade was prepared for her to argue again, or call them all stubborn idiots. He wasn't prepared for her next words.

"The only place I'll feel safe is with you. I don't trust an AI to protect me. I do trust all of you."

Veth. How could they argue with that? Apparently, his brothers felt the same way because they looked at each other in baffled silence.

Finally, Dirk spoke. "If you stay with us, you will have to do exactly what we say, the instant we say it."

She started to nod, but he cut her off.

"You have to mean it. If you hesitate or argue, someone could die. So before you say yes, you need to commit to what it means."

Alyson flinched. "I meant it last time."

"And yet, you wouldn't leave Royan when we told you to run." Dirk's fingers drummed out a staccato beat on the arm of his chair.

"He was bleeding!"

"And there you go, arguing again. If one of us is bleeding, are you going to try and save us, too? Ward's a killer. If you give him a chance, he's going to take you out."

Blade saw the hurt and unhappiness in Alyson's eyes and opened his mouth to say something to ease the tension. Before he could, her shoulders slumped and she bowed her head in defeat.

"I promise to do what you say without hesitation. I don't want to be the reason any of you get hurt. I get it. I do. I just wish there was some other way to end this beside an all-out war with someone who doesn't have any choice."

Unlike most of their kind, Blade and his brothers had never faced their brethren across a battlefield. This would be their first time standing against one of their own, and it wasn't sitting well with any of them. "He's got his mission, and he's compelled to complete it. There is no other way. At least, none we've been able to figure out."

"We've got two more days. Surely Victor will be awake by then and can give us more information. There might still be a way to resolve this," Alyson said.

It was what they were all hoping for, but so far, hope hadn't done them much good. Victor's injuries had proven to be more serious than first thought. He'd been shot and left for dead by someone who believed his injuries weren't survivable, even for a cyborg. The only reason Victor was still alive was because Lieksa had been on hand to initiate repairs to his damaged implants. After she had done all she could, Dr. Basque had put Victor into a medically-induced coma to give his brain time to heal. He'd live, but there would be no answers until Victor was awake again.

With time running out, they were left planning for the worst case scenario; the one where not everyone lived.

"If it comes to a choice between him or you, he'll die. Since you've made it clear you're not going to stay on the ship, there isn't going to be any margin for error. That's the price for what you want. You might have to watch us kill someone to save your life. I'm trying to protect you from that, but you won't let me." Dirk stomped out of the room before anyone could react to what he'd said.

"And there goes Officer Overkill," she huffed. "He says *I'm* stubborn. Has he looked in a damned mirror?"

"He doesn't have to." Lance pointed to himself, then Blade. "He's got us for that."

Blade understood what had Dirk so frustrated. He wanted to protect Alyson having to witness that kind of violence, too. They all did.

"True." Alyson chewed on her lip for a second, then sighed again. "So, since you're very much alike in some ways, do you share his opinion on what's best for me?"

Hello, slippery slope to Hell. Time for a distraction. "Uh, before we answer that, how mad are you going to be if we say yes?" he asked, giving her his best sad puppy face.

She flashed a glimmer of a smile, and he seized the moment. He sent a quick internal message to Lance and got to his feet. *"Follow my lead, or we're in as much trouble as Dirk."*

"I've got a better idea. Instead of rehashing things we've already talked about, how about we do something else?"

"You're avoiding my question," she pointed out.

Damn right he was. "Maybe. Or maybe I'm tired of talking and want to dance with you. We haven't danced yet, you know."

"You want to dance? Here?" Alyson gestured around the rec area. It was a moderate size, with well-worn chairs and a newer-looking lounge taking up most of the available space.

"For what I have in mind, this will work perfectly. Why don't you take a seat on the edge of that lounge, while Lance and I clear some space?"

"I can't decide if you're brilliant, or insane. Either way, you owe me a drink. We agreed to never discuss this again." Lance grumbled over their private channel.

"Would you rather answer her question?"

"Excellent point." Lance hopped up and started moving furniture.

"What about music?" Alyson asked.

"Right. Ship, display your musical library on the rec area's monitor. Eliminate any ballads and orchestral pieces."

It didn't take long to find a song that would work. He tapped the screen to make his selection and told the computer to begin playing the song in two minutes. That should give them enough time to call up their encoded memories of the last routine they'd done together. It wouldn't be a perfect performance, but it would be a memorable one.

"Ship, dim lights in the rec area to one-third normal." Lance had cleared the area around Alyson, giving them enough room to move.

"Am I part of this dancing plan, or am I supposed to stay seated?"

"You stay put for now. Remember when I told you that Lance I had worked a short stint as dancers? You're about to get a private performance."

"I am?" She settled deeper into her chair and beamed. "This should be fun. Where did you guys dance, anyway? You never said."

"Ever been to the Torex mining platform?" Lance asked.

"Only once. I recall it being a big, busy place where they process most of the ore coming in from the asteroid field. I briefly considered investing in one of the medical clinics there, but then I got the opportunity to buy the clinic on Astek outright."

"Did you see much of the lower concourse? That's where we worked. A hole in the wall called Grinding Rods. The whole bar was done up to look like a machinist shop, lots of gears and pistons and metal. The drinks were cheap, and the owner had dancers perform a few nights a week. Girls, guys, and aliens, we all had assigned nights."

"I never got down to the lower areas. I heard about it, though. Rough place full of rougher folks looking for a good time."

"That's the nicest description I've ever heard of the place. It was a cesspool, and we moved on as soon as we had the scrip to pay for transport to another part of the Drift." Blade took a moment to take off his shoes and socks, a move he instantly regretted when his bare feet hit the cold deck plating.

"You ready?" Lance asked, moving to stand in front of Alyson.

"Yep." Blade turned his attention to Alyson. "Only one rule. No moving. You stay right where you are, and keep your hands to yourself."

"That's two rules. And where's the fun if I have to sit still?" She demanded.

Lance chuckled. "Trust me, we'll make sure you enjoy yourself."

*

Alyson knew they were deliberately distracting her, and she was more than happy to let them. She'd talk to Dirk again after she had time to mull over what he had said. For now, she wanted to enjoy what little time they had left.

Blade and Lance were standing only a few feet in front of her, both of them grinning as the music started. She'd been to a few clubs with male dancers before, but she had never done more than watch from the back of the room. That wasn't going to be an option this time.

Both of them moved in time to the bass-heavy music. At first, it was nothing more than a slow roll of their hips, but as the beat sped up, so did they. Every step they took was in perfect synch, and every move was a display of sex appeal and strength.

They even stripped off their shirts at the same time, giving her an eyeful of hard muscle and bare skin. It was a sight she would never get bored of. When they moved in closer, she forgot the rules and reached for them, only to have Blade wag his finger at her and move back out of reach. While she watched him, Lance came around behind her. She didn't realize he was there until he grasped her arms and drew them gently behind her back.

"Ship, pause the music. What did we say about touching, sunshine? We really need to work on your ability to follow directions."

She laughed. "Good luck with that."

"Stubborn woman," he whispered in her ear as something warm was wrapped around her wrists.

She jerked at her arms, but there was no chance she could break free of Lance's hold unless he let her, and he wasn't going to.

"That is brilliant, and evil, brother of mine." Blade cupped her cheek and winked at her. "You look incredibly sexy right now, Doc."

Lance finished knotting what had to be his shirt around her wrists and came back into view. "Ship, restart the music."

"You're going to pay for this you know." She wriggled, testing how tight the knots were.

"If you want to tie me up and have your way with me later, you go right ahead."

They started to dance again, and the heat level kept rising with every seductive look and move. Her clit started to throb and her pussy grew slick with arousal as she watched them dance. Though it wasn't really dancing anymore, it was something more primal than that. It was sex without contact, and by the time the song reached the midpoint, she was aching to be touched.

She moved to the edge of her seat and leaned forward, hoping they'd take the hint.

Blade chuckled and strutted up to her, giving her a clear view of how turned on he was. His cock was a hard line straining against the cloth of his pants, and if she'd had her hands free, she would have helped him get them off.

"Untie me, please."

"Not yet." Lance took his brother's place in front of her. He was so close she could lean in and lick the sculpted ridge of his abs, but she managed to resist the temptation. Something told her the more she disobeyed, the longer they'd tease her.

He threaded his fingers through her hair, drawing her head back, so she was looking him in the eyes as he closed the distance between them. He pushed between her thighs, and she parted her legs, letting him in closer. He ground his body against hers, his cock rubbing across her breasts.

Delicious friction added fresh fuel to the fire already burning inside her, and she uttered a soft moan.

Within seconds, Blade was behind her, kneeling on the lounge so that his thighs were pressed to her back and the solid bulge of his cock was tight against her spine. They were still moving in time to the music, carrying her with them until the rhythm stole her reason and she gave in to it.

The next time Lance moved against her, she dipped her head and raked her teeth lightly across his stomach. He groaned, and then Blade moved in again, giving her a chance to reach up a little to stroke her fingers over his cock.

"You trying to tell us something?" Blade asked.

"Do you really need to ask?" she retorted, impatience putting an edge on her words. Her confidence had grown since their first time together; bolstered by their love and obvious desire for her. She'd never dared to take control though. Not until now.

"Tell us what you want us to do," Lance encouraged.

"I want my hands back, and your pants off. Both of you."

"And if you could only have one of those things, which would it be?" Blade asked, his voice a sexy rumble by her ear.

"The two of you naked."

"Our lady has spoken," Lance said.

"Clearly." Blade agreed.

She couldn't do anything but watch as they peeled off the rest of their clothes, somehow managing to keep to the beat of the new song that had started playing during their brief discussion.

Despite the fact her hands were still tied, Alyson was the one in control. "Now I want Lance to stand in front of me, and Blade, back behind me. Blade gets to use his hands." She arched a brow at Lance. "You don't."

Blade chortled in gleeful delight and moved in behind her. He had her shirt unbuttoned in a matter of seconds and cupped her breasts in his hands, working her nipples hard enough to make her gasp.

Lance stepped between her parted thighs, a cocky grin on his lips as he gazed down at her. "And what about me?"

She didn't bother answering him. Instead, she bowed her head and took the tip of his cock into her mouth. He groaned, and she felt his shaft pulse and harden.

"*Veth*, that feels good. Suck me just like that."

She started to hum softly as she explored every silken inch of him with the tip of her tongue. She took her time, lapping and circling the tip until his thighs were shaking and his breathing was ragged.

Blade never stopped touching her. He alternated between tender caresses and harder tweaks and tugs on her nipples, keeping her off-balance and turned on at the same time.

"Take him deeper," Blade murmured in encouragement.

"*Fraxx*, yes. Please. I want your mouth on me."

Instead of more, she gave him less, until the broad crown of his dick was barely resting against her lips.

"That's cruel," Lance muttered, but he went still and silent after that one grumbling complaint. That's all she had been looking for. Like her grandmother was fond of saying, what's sauce for the goose is sauce for the gander, too.

She didn't make him wait for long. After a few seconds, she lowered her head once more, working his cock with her lips and tongue until he was groaning her name and rocking his hips against her mouth. When he was close to coming, she leaned in and let him go deeper than she'd ever tried before.

He jerked his hips and cried out her name as his release tore through him, leaving him shuddering over her as she swallowed every drop. He was still struggling to catch his breath when she raised her head until his cock popped free and she flashed him a cocky grin of her own.

"My turn, now," was all he said.

He must have said something to Blade via their internal link, because the next thing she knew, the two of them were working together to lift her onto Lance's shoulder.

"This looks kind of familiar," Blade observed. "Only you're missing those cute fuzzy slippers this time."

"I didn't have time to pack those. And for *veth's* sake, why am I being carried like this again? I'm perfectly capable of walking!"

"Well, for one thing, this way is a lot more fun for us, sunshine."

"Not to mention it gives us a gorgeous view of your ass." Blade emphasized his point by leaning in and nipping one cheek.

She started swearing at them in every language she knew, well aware that cyborgs were fluent in all the languages in the galaxy and would understand every word she said.

They laughed at her all the way to their shared quarters, and by the time they set her back on her feet, she was laughing with them. That's one of the things she loved the most about her men: they made her laugh. No matter how dark things were, or how uncertain their future was, they never lost their sense of humor. She thought about Dirk and amended that thought. They never lost their sense of humor for long.

CHAPTER SIXTEEN

Lance gave his brother just enough time to untie Alyson's hands before he had her shirt off, closely followed by her pants and every other scrap of clothing she had on. He didn't stop until she was standing in front of him, naked and breathtakingly beautiful.

Without taking her eyes off him, she backed up until she bumped into the edge of the oversized bed that dominated the captain's quarters. "Is that where you want me?"

"Right smack in the middle of the bed is where I want you," Blade said.

"And then what?"

Lance looked at his brother. "Together?"

"Are you ready for that, Doc? Because if you are, all you have to do is say yes."

She held out a hand to each of them and smiled. "Yes."

Lance took her hand and drew her into his arms for a sizzling kiss as he made her a promise he knew he'd spend the rest of his life keeping. "I'd never do anything to hurt you."

"I know." She rose on her toes to kiss him, wrapping her slender arms around his neck as her tongue played hide-and-seek with his.

"This works better if we're all in the bed," Blade patted the empty bed beside him.

"He has a point," Alyson was laughing as she pulled out of Lance's arms and joined Blade.

"Shhh, don't encourage him." With Alyson now happily wrapped in Blade's arms, Lance took a moment to rummage through their collective clutter until he found what he was looking for; barrier gel. Part birth-control, part lube, it acted as a micro-thin barrier that allowed full sensation while protecting both partners from disease or pregnancy.

When he looked at Alyson again, she was riding Blade's fingers. Eyes closed, cheeks flushed, and her lips parted in a near-silent moan. "You couldn't wait for me, huh?"

"Nope. When I've got a beautiful woman in my arms, I'm not much for waiting."

Lance fisted his cock and settled in to enjoy the erotic display. Alyson was already primed and close to coming—he could tell by the way her breath caught and her hips rocked against Blade's hand. Every thrust and stroke of his fingers made her tremble a little more. Soon, her thighs were glistening, and her hips rose off the mattress in time to her greedy little moans.

"You're so *fraxxing* sexy when you're like this. All flushed and mussed and craving our touch. Do you want to come now, or do you want to wait until we're both inside you?"

"Together. I want it to be when we're together," she whispered.

Blade withdrew his hand and nudged her toward Lance. "I think Lance is looking a little lonely. Why don't you ride him while I get you ready?"

Lance's cock turned to stone in his hand, and he lay back on the bed, inviting her to join him. She came to him with a smile that lit up the room, straddling his hips and bracing her hands on his chest. When she leaned down to kiss him, he rocked his hips up at the same time, seating himself a few delicious inches inside her tight channel. She was ready and eager for him, pressing herself down until he was buried balls-deep. Her inner muscles flexed around his cock, milking him so hard he damn near came on the spot.

"Patience," he told her through gritted teeth. "We're only halfway to heaven."

"I'm not feeling very patient at the moment. I'm feeling greedy."

Then by all means, let me give you something to take the edge off." He slid his fingers down to where their bodies joined and started to work her clitoris between his fingers. He needed her to be relaxed and ready for what came next. "Just keep your eyes on me and focus on how good you feel right now. We're going to take good care of you."

She looked down at him with total trust and adoration, and he knew it was time.

"You're up," he told Blade.

*

Alyson did everything they'd taught her to do over the last few days as they had introduced her to some of the darker pleasures, including anal sex. She focused on the pleasure Lance was giving her and did her best not to tense as Blade started stroking his fingers down her spine and then lower still.

"Lean forward a little." Blade guided her into the position he wanted with a few gentle touches. She was so focused on him that she nearly forgot about Lance.

"Don't think, feel," Lance told her, reached up to take her hair in his hands, and dragged her down for a slow, deep kiss. She braced her hands on the bed by his shoulders and leaned down to kiss him back, letting their tongues dance together in a slow rhythm that he matched with each gentle rise and fall of his hips.

When Blade touched her again, she didn't tense. Not even when his slick fingers made their way along the seam of her ass. She let herself get lost in sensations, letting go of her worries and doubts until she was afloat in a sea of pleasure, rising and falling with each peak and wave that washed over her.

When a trickle of cool, slick liquid hit her fever-hot skin she gasped in surprise, then gasped again as Blade massaged her skin in slow, easy circles. The sensations grew more intense with every stroke, and soon she was rocking back and forth between the arch of Blade's hips and the touch of Lance's hand. By the time he finally pressed the tips of his fingers to her back entrance she was more than ready. There was a brief bite of pain when he pushed one finger inside, but it was quickly replaced by a burn that blurred the lines between pleasure and pain.

They worked together, kissing, stroking, and fucking her until she was half out of her mind with need. When Blade added a second finger, she moaned aloud and tightened her pussy walls around Lance's cock.

When Blade pulled out of her, she felt another burn, but this one was quickly cooled with another application of barrier gel.

"Hold still, sunshine," Lance whispered as Blade moved in tight behind her, lining up his cock and gently easing himself past the tight ring of muscle that guarded her back passage.

She couldn't have moved if her life depended on it. Her body was stretched to its fullest, and her mind was caught up in a tempest of sensations that threatened to overwhelm her.

"Veth, that's incredible," Blade said, his voice edged with barely restrained need.

Slowly, the dark pain transformed into pleasure, and Alyson finally exhaled.

"You okay?" Lance asked.

"So much better than okay." She felt like she could fly right now, leave the ship and soar among the stars.

Blade chuckled and gripped her hips. "I'm going to take that as an enthusiastic yes,"

She flexed around them both in response, and both of them started to move. Carefully at first, but as they found their rhythm, they moved faster and went deeper. There was nothing for her to do but hold on and try to remember to breathe as the pleasure built to a crescendo.

Both men whispered her name as they claimed her, and soon she couldn't tell the point where she stopped and they began. Her release started to blossom inside her, a firestorm of needs that had her crying out in wordless joy. She soared higher than she'd ever gone before, and before she could come back to earth, they both joined her. She could feel their cocks jerk and pulse inside her as they came, both of them shuddering with the force of their passion.

"I think you broke me, and I love you for it," Blade panted a few seconds later, his breath fanning over her back.

"You're amazing, love," Lance whispered, nuzzling her hair.

She was slumped on Lance's chest, still pinned between her lovers in an exhausted tangle of limbs. "That was...I don't have the words for it, but I hope we can do it again, soon."

"Anytime you want, sweetheart. You just say the word." Blade eased himself off of her and then flopped down on the bed at her side.

She reached out for his hand and wove their fingers together. "Soon."

She closed her eyes and settled her head on Lance's chest so that his heartbeat was a soothing thump against her ear. This was how she wanted to spend every night for the rest of their lives: tangled up with her men, breathless, happy, and loved. "I love you guys so much. But it doesn't scare me anymore. Now, all that scares me is the thought of losing you."

Both men shook their heads.

"We've only just got you into our lives," Lance said.

"So don't start thinking that we're going anywhere, anytime soon. You're stuck with us, Doc."

She closed her eyes and let herself drift. "I like the sound of that...very much."

* * * *

Alyson walked past the galley where Lance and Blade were arguing over what to have for dinner, but she didn't join them. There was someone else she wanted to see, and he had been keeping his distance.

She had given Dirk until she got out of the shower to reappear, but when she asked the AI for his location and learned he was still hiding in the cockpit, she knew that she would have to go to him. She ran a brush through her still-damp hair, grabbed one of the guys' T-shirts to wear, and set off to beard the grumpy lion in his electronic den.

Her sock-clad feet made no noise as she padded down the dimly lit corridor that led to the cockpit. Her silent approach allowed her to hear the conversation going on ahead of her. Dirk was talking to someone, and since both of his brothers were in the galley, he had to be talking to their friends back at Astek Station.

"If he remembers anything else, you'll let me know?" Dirk asked.

"If any of us think of something that can help, you know we'll be in touch."

She recognized Toro's deep voice and hurried the last few feet. It sounded like Victor was finally awake. What had he told them? Did he know a way to stop his brother? She had a thousand questions to ask.

"We'll talk again, soon. I need to round up the others and let them know what's going on. For now, thanks, and we'll be in touch."

Toro and several other familiar voices said a brief goodbye, and by the time she got to the doorway the call was over.

"Hey, squishy. Did I hear you talking with Toro a second ago?"

It was a testament to his level of worry that he didn't react to his new nickname.

"You did." Dirk spun the chair around and opened his arms. "Come here."

One look at his face and everything she had intended to say got pushed aside. It could wait until she learned what had marked his face with worry lines and put the shadows in his clear green eyes.

She curled up in his lap and tried not to smile when he snuggled her in close and uttered a near-silent sigh of contentment. "Tell me."

"Good news first. Victor's awake and is going to be fine. There are still some gaps in his memory, but he was able to give us more information."

"I'm glad he's going to be okay. I should have been there to help." She sighed in frustration. "I hate being out here. I'm no use to anyone like this."

"This is temporary. You'll be back to saving lives and doing the impossible soon enough. By leaving the station, you made sure no one else got hurt." Dirk tweaked a strand of her hair. "Stop beating yourself up over making a hard choice."

"Good advice. Any chance you're going to apply it to yourself, too?"

He uttered a frustrated grunt. "Maybe."

"You weren't wrong. Before, I mean. If I'm with you three, I might have to see you kill someone. But, I've seen death before, and if it were a choice between your life and someone else's, I'd make the same decision." She laid a hand on his cheek and turned his head so he was looking straight at her. "Seeing your violent side isn't going to make me feel any differently about you. I love you, and that's never going to change."

"I'd rather you never saw that part of us."

"Love is messy. We don't get to pick which parts of a person we want to love, and reject the rest. I've seen what kind of man you are, Dirk. And I love him. Grumpy bits and all.

"Lance is right. You see us differently than everyone else does. Why is that?"

"I grew up with parents who viewed everything through a filter that valued people by what they could do for them. Favours. Money. Influence. Connections. They saw everything that way, including their children. My grandparents showed me there was more to people than that, and encouraged me to look closer before judging someone's worth."

"How anyone could miss seeing your worth is a mystery to me." He gave her a slow, easy smile that lessened the worry that clouded his eyes.

"You see it. That's enough for me." She kissed him softly, then turned the conversation back to more serious matters. "Now that we're talking again, do you want to tell me the bad news Toro gave you?"

"The Reaper got away. They did a complete inventory of all ships docked at the station and figured out which one was theirs, so at least we know what ship to watch for."

"We already figured he'd come after me." She smoothed a finger over his furrowed brow. "So, what's the really bad news?"

"He may not be the only one on board. Apparently, they had a handler, Ariel Coal.

At least, that's the name they knew her by. Mack's certain it's an alias and has sent your friend Phaedra deep-diving into cyberspace to figure out who she really is, and who she's working for."

"And we don't know if she's with him or not?"

"She's not on the station anymore. That's all we know right now. We have to assume she's with Ward. It was her job to make sure they stayed compliant and on target. If she's with him, then our plans have to change. You need to stay with us—you're not going to be safe anywhere else."

"Damn right I need to stay with you." She smiled and kissed him. "Stop worrying so much."

"I'll stop worrying when Ward and his handler are dealt with and we're on our way home." Dirk went silent for a long moment, but something in his expression told her not to press him. Eventually, he spoke again. "There's more. Vic said that he and his brother were controlled using an override command. If they showed any sign of awareness or resisted orders, she'd use the command, and they'd lose consciousness. When they woke up, they'd be back under her control. It would take a while for awareness to begin again, and the cycle would repeat."

Horror turned her blood ice cold and sent a chill chasing down her spine. "They…they can do that?"

"Until a few minutes ago, I would have said no. But…" He shrugged his broad shoulders.

"But apparently they can. Whoever *they* are. Does Victor know who he was working for? What was the code? Can we use it?" Not that she liked the idea of shutting down another being's mind, but it was a better alternative than having to kill Ward.

"They're working on a way to retrieve the code from his memories. There's a block in place that prevents him from being able to say or write it. The bastards covered their asses on that one. He doesn't know who their handler reported to. They were given a target and sent after it. Everyone thought they were working for the cartels, but the cartels wouldn't know how to reprogram a cyborg. They had to have corporation help."

Re'veth. Every time she thought the corporations couldn't get any viler, they went and proved her wrong.

"They'd need more than simple support. They'd need someone with the skills and training to implant new programming. Somewhere out there, a corporation, or at least part of one, has gone totally rogue."

It was a sickening thought. Corporations defying the law, missing cyborgs, secret override commands, cyborgs taken and turned back into weapons against their will. It had to stop.

"This started out so simple. Reverse what the corporations had done to the cyborg women. How did I end up in the middle of all this? This is so much bigger than any of us could have imagined."

"It is. But I don't regret getting involved. Blade, Lance, and I, we're finally part of something important. Protecting you, helping our brethren. This feels right."

"As insane as that sounds, I agree with you. But I'm not so crazy that I don't wish we had a little more help dealing with Ward and this Coal woman."

"Did I forget to mention that the IAF is sending a ship our way? Unfortunately, it won't get here before Ward does. By the time there was actionable intel for our friends back home to hand over, there wasn't enough time for even their fastest ships to make the trip."

"So, all you three have to do is keep me, and yourselves, alive until the IAF arrives."

"Yeah, that's all. "

"I have faith in you." She whispered before leaning in to kiss him. He hadn't shaved for a few days. It made him look even more like his brothers and added a rough edge to his appearance.

"I'm glad, but I'm still going to worry."

"I'm going to be fine. I have you protecting me."

"There's something you could do to help me worry a little less. Take the medi-bots Zale gave you. It's time, Alyson. They might save your life."

"I..." She paused. There really wasn't any reason she couldn't do it now. Save for the fact she hadn't thought to pack the injector during her five-minute packing session. It was still on her desk back home.

"I don't have it with me. I never even thought about it. We had to get out of there so quickly."

He reached into his pocket and pulled out the pre-loaded injector. "When I went to get your medical bag, I grabbed this, too."

"What would I do without you?"

"I hope neither of us has to live without the other for a very long time." He lifted the injector. "If you do this, you're going to live as long as we will. I want..." He cupped the back of her head in his hand and stared into her eyes. "I want to spend that life together, Alyson."

She reached up and gently guided his hand and the injector to the side of her throat, directly over her jugular vein. "My life is so much better now that I've finally let you three into it. I don't want this to end."

"We should probably make this official at some point. You know, a ring, a ceremony, a cake and lots of drinks, but for now, this will have to do." He pressed the injector against her skin and pressed the trigger.

She barely felt the sting as nanites entered her bloodstream. Her heart and head were too busy reacting to what he'd said. "Did you propose to me while you were shooting me full of tech?"

He grinned. "That depends on your answer."

Her heart sang, and she was laughing as she answered. "You can't take it back because my answer is yes. It's too soon, and we could all die tomorrow, and I have no idea how to be married to three men at once, but yes. I must be crazy."

"You're our kind of crazy. That's all that matters."

There was a clang as the now-empty injector hit the deck and then his lips crashed down on hers. Euphoria and desire came together with the force of a comet strike. His hands slid under her shirt to lay claim to bare skin, and she did the same to him. Soon, they'd tell the others the good news, but not yet. She had already shared something special with Lance and Blade. This time was for Dirk.

This was what it would be like for the rest of her life; sharing herself with three men who all owned a piece of her heart. The thought made her laugh.

"What's funny?" Dirk demanded.

"I was thinking that if I'm going to spend the rest of my days with the three of you, I'm not going to get much sleep."

"Thanks to the medi-bots you've now got running through your veins, you don't need to sleep for more than a few hours at a time." His grin grew wicked. "Imagine all the extra time we're going to have."

"If I didn't know better, I might think that was the real reason you wanted me to take that shot. And here I thought Blade was the sex-obsessed one."

"We're clones, Aly. There are some differences because we spent time apart, but deep down, we're very much alike." Dirk took her hand and pressed it over the hard bulge of his cock to make his point clear.

"You're three of a kind. *My* three." She nipped his lower lip and deftly unfastened his pants, wrapping her fingers around his thick shaft the moment it was free.

"I've got a better idea. Hang on," he told her, his eyes aglow with lust and a hint of laughter.

She threw her arms around his neck and held on as he rose to his feet, taking her with him. "Where are we going?"

"Not far. Legs around my waist."

She twined her legs around his hips and locked her ankles at the small of his back. He walked to the bulkhead at the rear of the cockpit, not stopping until she was pressed up against the cold metal surface.

The sharp chill of the metal behind her contrasted with the heat of his body where they touched. Especially the point where his steel-hard cock was trapped between them. He kissed her again, rocking his hips in time to the thrust and parry of his tongue as he slid his cock back and forth across her fast-slickening pussy. He lifted her a little higher, and her labia parted, letting him stroke directly over her clit.

"Again. Do that again." She bucked her hips, trying to increase the pressure.

He groaned and pushed in deeper, grinding their bodies together until they were both shaking with need.

"Want you," she whispered when she couldn't take another minute without him inside her.

*

Dirk knew he was being greedy, keeping Alyson to himself, but he wanted to have this moment alone with her. She'd just agreed to be his for the rest of her life. *His. Theirs. Ours. Forever.*

He kissed her again as he shifted her warm weight in his arms, lifting her until the tip of his dick was lined up at her entrance. He filled her slowly, taking his time to enjoy every second of pleasure that came as her body gave way to his.

He had her ass in the palms of his hands, holding her against the wall with the weight of his body. Clothes still half on, limbs tangled, her scent was all around them, wrapping him in a cocoon of bliss.

"You're mine," he panted as he drew back and then drove deep inside her. "Mine to protect. Mine to love." His claims were timed to the thrust of his hips, each one deeper than the last until he was fully sheathed in her sweet heat.

Her soft cries of need pushed him to the ragged edge of his control and words quickly failed him. Her nails scored his back, hard enough to sting even through the shirt he still wore. She was a wild thing in his arms, arching and scratching, her cries ringing down the corridor of the ship as she rode him hard.

There was no way his brothers would stay away for long. Their moment was coming to an end. He moved faster, abandoning any pretense of control as he took her in a series of hard, deep thrusts that had her inner walls squeezing tight around his cock.

There were footsteps coming toward them now, but he was too far gone to care. Nothing mattered but the two of them and the pleasure they shared. His cock thickened and his balls tightened as his orgasm hit hard enough to steal his breath and fill his vision with a thousand dancing stars. She milked every ounce of cum from his balls and then bowed her head to muffle her cries of ecstasy against his shoulder.

They were still locked together in the blissful aftermath of their lovemaking when his brothers erupted into the cockpit, crowding into the doorway at the same time.

"The wall? This ship has beds, Dirk. You couldn't wait long enough to find one of them?" Blade asked.

"We were celebrating, and no, we couldn't wait that long," Alyson replied pertly.

Lance's eyebrows nearly hit his hairline. "Celebrating what, exactly?"

"I'm bulletproof now. Well, almost."

"She finally agreed to inject the medi-bots." Dirk tweaked her nose. "Which is not the same thing as being bulletproof. Medi-bots don't block pain, remember? So, no acts of reckless bravery."

"Yeah, that's my job," Blade added.

Alyson wiggled in his arms. "You should probably put me down now. I need to go find more clothes, and you…" She grinned. "You might want to tell your brothers what else I agreed to."

He withdrew from her body and set her back on her feet. He took a moment to adjust both their clothing, so they were more or less respectable.

Alyson paused just long enough to kiss both his brothers and then squeezed past them into the corridor. "Break it to them gently, but remember, no takebacks!"

"What did you do?" Lance demanded.

"More importantly, are we going to have to kick your ass for whatever it is?" Blade added.

"I uh, might have proposed to Alyson while I was injecting her with the nanites."

They stared at him in unblinking shock.

Lance burst out laughing. "What is it about our woman that breaks all your *fraxxing* filters?"

"No kidding. First, you tell her you love her before we even start our first date, and now this? She's broken you, Dirk."

He knew that wasn't true. "She didn't break me. She made me whole. We've talked about this before. She's the one. She's always been the one."

Both of them nodded, but it was Lance who spoke first. "That's true. Which means when this is over we'll need to ask her again. All three of us."

Blade poked his finger into Dirk's chest. "And you don't get to say a damned word this time, mister I-already-proposed. I'm supposed to be the impetuous one, remember?"

"Like I was telling Aly earlier, we're clones. Deep down, we're very much alike." He grinned at his brother. "I've just got a little more restraint than you two clowns."

"Except when it comes to Alyson," Lance and Blade said in unison.

He nodded. "When it comes to her, all bets are off."

CHAPTER SEVENTEEN

The time for planning was over.

Blade had so much adrenaline coursing through his veins he was on the verge of vibrating. Ward's ship had appeared on long range scanners hours ago, and they had the *Sprite's* AI tracking his approach and relaying the information to them in real time.

They were gathered near the center of what remained of the automated resupply station, though it was in such rough shape that calling it a space station was a stretch. Phaedra had been right about there being an active AI and breathable atmosphere, but she hadn't mentioned the AI's program had degraded to the point it was downright temperamental and prone to fits of irrational behavior.

Even the newest resupply stations were little more than a place to store parts, goods, and supplies until they could be sold to long haul crews who had no other option but to pay exorbitant prices for the simplest items. The station they were on was far from new. It had been abandoned for years, maybe even decades. The AI that ran the place couldn't even tell them how long it had been in operation.

There were entire levels of the station where the hull integrity had failed, leaving it open to the vacuum of space. Judging by the scorch marks and damage, not all of the failures had been structural. The station had either been used for firing practice, or it had been involved in at least one full-scale firefight.

They'd chosen one of the internal storage bays as the place to make their stand. It was a wide-open space with a pair of massive double doors at one end, and no other access points, at least not once they finally convinced the AI to lock down the ventilation tunnels on the whole level.

They'd spent hours hauling whatever loose debris and furniture they could find down to the bay to form a series of barricades. Everything from tables and chairs to massive pieces of broken machinery and replacement parts had been piled up. The only way they'd managed it in time was by lowering the gravity enough to be able to push the damned things around, but it had worked. The obstacles would act as a funnel, directing Ward to them through a maze that would maximize their chances of ending this without bloodshed.

Their attempt to bring this to a happy end would have been a long shot, but last night they'd received a heavily encrypted message with some good news that gave them hope. Thanks to the work of Lieksa and the others, a way had been found to work around Victor's program blocks and obtain the override code that would render Ward unconscious. It was nothing more than a couple of innocuous nonsense words, but they'd been assured it would work.

The plan was simple. Get Ward to come to them and find a way to bring him down, unhurt if possible. Alyson would park her ass behind a second barrier at the far end of the bay, as far from the door as possible. She was the cheese in the trap, but there was no chance in hell any of them were going to let Ward get anywhere near her.

"Ship, scan the incoming vessel again and report all life signs." Dirk had made the same request numerous times since Ward's ship had appeared on the scanners.

"One lifeform detected."

The answer hadn't varied, but they needed to be sure. Ward's handler was still out there, somewhere, and she was an unknown variable.

"He seems to be alone." Alyson was pacing the space behind her designated shelter. Her normal serenity was gone, replaced by a need to stay in constant motion. Blade felt the same way.

"She might have left the ship after they left the Drift, or she might have never been on board at all. I wish we knew for sure." Lance was leaning up against a chunk of rusted machinery. His hand rested on his holstered blaster and his eyes were on the doorway despite the fact they still had a few minutes left.

"Or she could be there with him, and one of them is hidden from our sensors. According to Zura, the *Sun Sprite's* cargo bay is specially designed to deflect scans. It's possible they're both on that ship."

Dirk was the only one of them that appeared calm, but Blade knew it was an illusion. He was as tightly wound as everyone else. A calm man wouldn't be wearing the arsenal of blasters, blades, and weaponry that Dirk, and the rest of them, were outfitted with. Even Alyson was armed. She'd learned basic firearm handling from her grandfather, and after a few quick lessons in how the more advanced weaponry worked, she was ready to go. Their plans didn't include her ever needing to defend herself, but what plan survived contact with the enemy?

Once they had confirmation that Ward's ship was docked, they took their positions. They weren't hiding. Finding them would be easy, and that was the point. Ward's only advantage was the shield device he carried. With it activated, he'd be damned near invisible. To nullify that advantage, they were forcing Ward to come to them.

Blade's sole job was to watch the doorway and let the others know when Ward was inside the maze. He would scan for heat signatures and any other sign he could see that their target had arrived.

Five minutes passed. Then ten. The tension mounted with every second that ticked past. *Where the* fraxx *was he?*

A faint footfall broke the silence. It was barely audible, even to Blade's enhanced hearing, but it was enough to confirm they weren't alone. Ward was in the corridor outside.

He tightened his grip on his blaster and waited. A painfully long minute later, there was another noise. This one much louder.

"Did he just trip? Whoever heard of a clumsy assassin?" Lance asked via their internal comm channel, and Blade had to fight the urge to snicker. On the heels of that reaction came another one; this guy was too good to screw up like this. Something was off.

Before he could relay his thoughts to the others, the target appeared in the bay doors. *Fraxx.* He didn't have his shield activated. Nothing about this felt right.

Still, he stuck to the plan. It was too late to ad lib now, anyway. Once Ward passed his position, Blade would move in behind him, sealing off his only escape route.

Ward walked into the bay as if he were taking a stroll through a meadow instead of stepping into an obvious trap. As he passed by, Blade got his first real look at their target. He was definitely related to Jaeger and Toro. Same dark coloring, similar features, and there was something about the faint smile on his lips that reminded Blade of Toro when the big man was fighting in the Nova Club cage matches.

It wasn't a friendly smile.

Two steps into the maze, Ward started to whistle. It was a slow, eerie tune that sounded vaguely familiar. It took a few more bars before Blade recognized it: "Ring Around the Rosie," slowed down to a dirge-like pace.

"Guy sure knows how to make an entrance. Once he rounds that next bend, I'm moving in," Lance sent the message to his brothers.

"Stay sharp," Dirk replied.

They all focused on Ward as he made his way through the maze. Once he reached the designated spot, they went into action. Blade slipped through one of the carefully hidden gap in the barricades, raised his gun and waited.

Lance popped his head up only a few feet away from Ward. "Hey there, Ward. I've got a message for you. Your batch brothers, Jaeger and Toro, want you to come home."

Ward didn't respond. He turned and fired, but Lance had already dropped back behind the barricade.

The moment he turned and fired, Dirk made his move. In a loud, clear voice he spoke the tongue-twisting override code that Victor had given them. "Uthvas baythad."

It was as if they'd flicked a switch off in his brain. Ward dropped to the deck in a lifeless heap, and all of them stared in horror. What the *fraxx* had been done to him? Could they do it to any cyborg?

"We need to secure him. Fast. He should be out for hours, but we can't be sure," Lance said, reappearing from behind the barricade.

"Is it over? Are you all okay?" Alyson called out.

"We're fine. Stay put until we've got Ward secured," Lance called back as he started helping Blade stretch Ward out on the floor so they could bind him.

*

Alyson breathed a sigh of relief. It might not be over yet, but it should be soon. Her men were safe, and they'd managed to capture Ward without hurting him. Things were working out better than she'd dared to hope.

Somewhere on the other side of her makeshift wall, someone tripped. They landed against the barricade with a muffled curse that sounded distinctly feminine.

Adrenaline dumped into Alyson's veins. She wasn't alone. She shot to her feet, snatching her gun out of its holster and pointing it at…nothing.

"This was too easy." A woman's voice came out of nowhere.

There was a flash of red light, a searing pain, and Alyson staggered backward into the back wall of the storage bay. Pain tore through her, too much for even the adrenaline to block.

That's when she finally saw it. A shimmer in the air. A shield. Ignoring the agony radiating from her hip, Alyson lifted her blaster and fired. According to Vic, the shield could only absorb the energy from one shot.

She'd just have to stay alive long enough to shoot her attacker twice.

The shield distorted, flickered, and died, leaving Alyson face to face with a sharp-faced woman with dark hair and a sneer on her lips. The sneer rapidly faded as the woman realized what was happening.

"Stupid *fraxxing* tech!" She slapped at a small device clipped to her waist, but all it did was buzz and sizzle.

"Don't move." It took all her will to push herself off the wall and back onto her feet, but Alyson made herself do it while keeping her gun pointed at the woman standing on the other side of the barricade.

She heard the hammering approach of footsteps as two of her protectors charged across the storage bay.

"Put the weapon down and then raise your hands in the air." Dirk barked the order as he drew his blaster and pointed it at Ariel.

Ariel didn't move, but the sneer returned to her face as she uttered two strange words. "Ked Vada."

"I don't know what the hell you said, but unless it means 'I surrender,' you should probably shut up and put the weapon down. This is your last warning," Blade said.

Dirk glanced over at her and his gun dropped as he saw she was injured. "Alyson! Dammit, you're hit. I thought I told you not to let that happen."

Alyson was still trying to think of a snappy comeback when she spotted Ariel's blaster move. There wasn't time to shout a warning, so she didn't bother. Instead, Alyson snapped her own gun up and fired at Ariel just as the woman took her shot.

More blaster fire sounded, and then everything went quiet. It was over.

At least, she thought it was. Pain made it hard to think clearly, and even the smallest movement hurt, but she managed to stay upright. There was a body on the ground, and it only took a second for her to be sure that it didn't belong to either Blade or Dirk. Relieved, she sagged against the wall as the last of her energy drained away. The blaster fell from her nerveless fingers and another wave of agony washed over her. This time, she didn't try to fight it. She let herself slide down the wall until she reached the floor.

Dirk raced to her side and dropped to the floor beside her. "How bad is it?"

"Hurts, but I'll live," she replied through gritted teeth. "The others?"

"We're fine. She missed. You didn't," Blade said.

"Lance?"

"He stayed behind to secure Ward. He's fine."

It was hard to think past the pain, but Alyson needed to know what was going on. "Is she dead?"

"Very."

"Good." She should probably feel guilty for killing the other woman, but right now, she couldn't muster that kind of compassion for someone who had tried to take her life and the lives of the people she loved.

Dirk checked her wound, muttering under his breath at the damage.

"I'll live, right?"

"Yeah." He stretched out beside her and eased an arm around her shoulders, drawing her in close. "Nice shooting back there. You know, if you ever decide to give up being a doctor, I think you might have what it takes to be a hell of a bodyguard."

"Thanks." She sucked in a breath and raised her head enough to take a look at her injury. She'd taken a blaster bolt to the hip, low enough to partially miss the body armor they'd insisted she wear. A few inches higher, and she'd be in a lot better shape right now.

"She wasn't much of a shot, was she?" Alyson gently touched the edges of the wound. It was already healing, thanks to her new medi-bots, but it was still going to be painful for the next few hours.

"Apparently not, which is something I will be forever grateful for. If she'd been a better shot, you and Blade might not be with us right now." Dirk's voice caught as he looked at her injured side. "We failed you."

"I'm alive. Ward's alive. The bitch who messed with us is dead. I'm calling this a win."

"I love it when you get all bloodthirsty. How you feeling, Doc?" Blade joined them behind the barricade, crouching down at her feet with a worried smile on his face.

"Like I got shot. Any chance one of you wants to go get my medical bag from the ship? I could use a pain blocker."

His smile widened a little. "If you can still manage sarcasm, I guess that means you're going to be fine. And your bag's already here. Lance brought it down just in case things didn't go according to plan."

"I owe Lance a kiss for that. How's Ward?" she asked.

"Out cold and secure. We'll take him with us when we head back to the *Sun Sprite*. There isn't much we can do for him, but we can keep him comfortable until the IAF gets here."

"I hope they understand he's a victim in all this. The guilty one is over there." She nodded toward the corpse of Ward's handler.

"They know," Lance assured her, arriving with her bag and handing it to Dirk.

"What was that she said at the end? Did any of you understand her?" Alyson asked as Dirk rummaged through the bag for a pain blocker.

All three of her men shook their heads.

"It wasn't in any language we're programmed with," Dirk said.

Blade's expression clouded into one of disturbed concern. "I think—I hate to even say it—but I think it was another override command. One she thought would affect us."

"I think so, too. I saw her face when she said it. She thought something would happen, something that would help her."

"We'll talk about this later." Dirk placed an injector loaded with pain blocker to her thigh and pressed the trigger.

Within seconds, the pain started to ebb, and soon she was floating on a comfortable cloud. She settled back into Dirk's arms and let herself drift.

"You ready to get out of here?" one of them asked.

She nodded. "More than ready."

Once Dirk was standing she reached out for Lance and Blade. "I love you three so much. I couldn't have done this without you."

"We love you too, sunshine." Lance squeezed her hand.

"Then take me home." She liked the way that sounded. Home, to a place where she was welcomed and needed. A place filled with friends who had her back, and three amazing men who were sworn to love and protect her. Home had never sounded so good.

EPILOGUE

Alyson looked around the table and smiled as she counted her many blessings. They were back in the Nova Club for a well-earned night of celebration, surrounded by friends that were more like family. The cyborgs, their allies, her staff from the clinic, even a few of the Intersellar Armed Forces officers who were part of the investigation team were here tonight.

It was the first time they had all been together since the *Sun Sprite's* return to the Drift, and it was the last night she'd see some of them for a while. Tomorrow, Phaedra, Nya, Zale, and his cousin Denz would be leaving on an IAF cruiser to take part in what everyone hoped would be a rescue mission. If everything went well, they'd be coming back with the missing cyborgs. The ones the corporations were still denying existed.

Well, most of the corporations. Some of them had seen the writing on the wall. Astek had been the first to quietly hand over their files while maintaining a public front of denial. Others were coming forward now, and the stack of evidence was growing into a mountain that would eventually bury the guilty ones.

The investigation was so big that the IAF was establishing a base out here in the Drift. For now, they were working out of Astek station, who had been exonerated early on. Soon though, a new station would be brought in to add to the Drift. The Interstellar Armed Forces were settling in for a long stay.

"I haven't seen you smile this much in well, forever, actually." Phaedra dropped into an empty seat at her side and set down two glasses on the battered tabletop, pushing one of them toward Alyson.

"Torskian Ale? Are you trying to kill me? I tried that stuff while I was away. My liver has yet to forgive me."

"Drink up, you wuss. You've got medi-bots in your bloodstream. You can't get a hangover." Phaedra raised her glass and grinned before taking a swig. "And now, neither can I."

"Zale?"

"Zale. Bless him and his magical nanotech."

Alyson nodded to a distant corner of the Club, where a rugged-looking older man in a perfectly fitted IAF uniform was sitting with several other officers. Since arriving on the station, Colonel Archer had made his presence known, but so far he had been mostly supportive of the cyborgs and their cause. "I thought the Colonel had banned him from producing anymore until they got things under control?"

Phaedra shrugged. "By the time Colonel bossy brass set foot on this station, Zale had already ensured we'd all gotten a dose. He wanted to be certain we were all protected. Not all of us have an entire team of sexy bodyguards to keep us safe."

At the mention of her men, Alyson glanced over in their direction. They were back to their normal, relaxed selves, laughing and drinking with Phylomenia Harrington and Royan. Captain Phyl had only arrived back at Astek station this morning, and no doubt she had a lot of questions about what had gone on while she had been on her last cargo run. She was the group's official den mother, dispensing advice and ass-kickings as needed, and they all loved her.

Phaedra tapped her glass against Alyson's. "No matter how long you stare at them, they can't get any hotter, you lucky woman."

"I am lucky, aren't I?" She finally tore her attention away from her men to look at her friend. It was hard to believe she was leaving tomorrow, but Phaedra didn't like staying in one place too long. Her past had a way of catching up to her. She'd be safe enough with the IAF, and once she had learned about the missing cyborgs, she'd pestered the Colonel until he had finally agreed to let her go along. They might need her unique skills where they were going: a secret base where Victor and Ward claimed they had seen the captives.

"Who knows, maybe I'll find myself some sexy cyborgs on this mission. Those IAF officers look damned fine in their uniforms. If I'm lucky, I'll get to find out what they look like out of them."

"You worry less about getting laid and more about staying in one piece. This could be dangerous. We have no idea what those bastards did to the cyborgs. They could be fine, or they might be like Vic and Ward." "You worry less about getting laid and more about staying in one piece. This could be dangerous. We have no idea what those bastards did to the cyborgs. They could be fine, or they might be like Vic and Ward." Astek had given the IAF confirmation that there were failsafe command words, like the one used to control Vic and Ward, programmed into the cyborgs. Astek swore they had deactivated that element from all of their cyborgs before they were released. Apparently, some of the other corporations hadn't done so.

Phaedra sighed. "How are those two doing? I know they're both out of custody, but I don't see them here tonight."

"They're not ready. At least, that's what Toro said when I asked. I can't imagine what they've been through, but it's going to take them time to work through it."

Phaedra nodded. "Not to mention, coming here tonight would mean meeting more than one person they were assigned to kill at one point or another. Talk about awkward."

Alyson had already visited Victor. It *had* been awkward, but she didn't blame either of them for what they'd done. After all, Victor's warning saved her life, and since his recovery he had taken the time to show the others how he and his brother had gotten around the station without being detected. Thanks to him, Astek station was more secure, and so was her clinic.

He'd explained to the others how his memories and his free will had started to return after he spotted his batch brothers in the Nova Club one night. He'd been following one of the Reaper's assigned targets to gain intel when he saw them. He had managed to hide his growing awareness from his handler, and when they were assigned a new target, he'd risked his life to alert Alyson to the danger while doing all he could to break Ward's mind free.

When Ariel finally figured out what Victor had done, she sent Ward to intercept Alyson. Once his brother was gone, she'd told Victor he was a liability and shot him.

Fortunately for everyone, her aim was lousy and he'd survived.

"Your smile is fading. Do I need to call your protection detail over here?" Phaedra asked.

"Sorry, I was thinking about Vic and Ward, and their bitch of a handler. I'm not sorry she's dead, but I do regret that we couldn't get any information out of her. We still don't know who she worked for. That information might help you guys when you get to this base."

"We'll figure it out. That Colonel is a pain in the ass, but he's motivated. I heard he's got Nova Force looking into the whole thing about what the Vault of the Fallen is, and how someone got access to their DNA. He's beyond pissed about that."

A niggling thought struck Alyson. "You are not hacking his comms, are you, Phae?"

Phaedra blue eyes widened in an attempt to make her look innocent. "Me? I'd never do such a thing."

"You're insane. Just once, could you try to behave yourself?"

"I don't want to behave myself. I want to make a difference, the way you have." She raised her glass and pointed to where Cynder stood, having a quiet conversation with Nya. "You changed their lives, Princess."

"You do make a difference. I wouldn't be here without you."

Phae grinned. "That's very true. If I hadn't stepped in, you would have married that Bryce idiot without ever knowing he was cheating on you, and then you wouldn't be engaged to marry those three sex gods in black leather over there."

Alyson looked down at the set of stacking rings on her left hand and grinned. They had asked her last night. All three of them on their knees and their words carefully timed so that they spoke in perfect synch. When she said yes, each of them had opened their hand to reveal three identical rings designed to be worn together. The narrow gold bands were set with three small, square-cut diamonds, and they had slipped them onto her finger one after another.

As if aware of her gaze, Dirk turned to look at her with that slow, sexy smile that she loved. A moment later all three of them were headed her way.

"And here they come. That's it, I'm out of here. I'm happy for you, but I'm not equipped to deal with the level of mushiness that is about to ensue." Phaedra drained her glass and leaned over to hug Alyson. "I'm off to find more booze and some trouble. Wish me luck."

"Love ya. I'll be at the docking arm tomorrow to see you off."

"You'd better be!" Phae headed off to the bar, her pink hair glowing in the strobing lights of the club.

"Hello, sunshine." Lance reached her first, setting down his drink and sweeping her off her chair and into his arms. She was wrapped up in warm leather and strength as he held her close and kissed her without restraint or a care for their audience.

By the time she was spun into Dirk's waiting arms, the room had erupted into cheers and laughter. His kiss was scorching, one hand on her ass, pulling her in hard as he laid claim to her mouth with his.

"She's wearing my ring, too, you know," Blade finally complained when Dirk showed no signs of letting her go.

Laughing, Dirk released her into Blade's embrace. "Good things come to those who wait."

"And I'm definitely a good thing," she added before Blade's lips were on hers. He didn't stop with a kiss, or two, or three. Tongues danced, lips mated--he kissed her until she was breathless and trembling in his arms.

"You are the best thing that's ever happened to me," he whispered against her lips before finally lifting his head again.

"The best thing that's happened to any of us." Dirk moved in behind her and Lance claimed a spot at her side as their friends all laughed and catcalled from around the bar.

She was too happy to care that she was making a scene. From somewhere in the shadows, she heard Anne calling out "And it's about time too!"

Alyson laughed with joy. Anne was right. It was about time she allowed herself to be happy. Tonight, they were celebrating all the good that had happened in the last few months. They'd achieved so much. Though there was more work to do and undoubtedly more threats to face, she wasn't going to face them alone. She had three of the bravest guardians in the cosmos watching over her, encouraging her, and loving her.

She'd put her life in their hands, and they'd given her their hearts in return.

THE END

ABOUT THE AUTHOR

Susan lives out on the Canadian west coast surrounded by open water, dear family, and good friends. She's jumped out of perfectly good airplanes on purpose and accidently swum with sharks on the Great Barrier Reef.

If the world ends, she plans to survive as the spunky, comedic sidekick to the heroes of the new world, because she's too damned short and out of shape to make it on her own for long.

To contact her about her books or to arrange end of the world team-ups, you can email her at *susan@susanhayes.ca.*

For all titles by Susan Hayes, or to sign up for ner newsletter, please visit her website: **susanhayes.ca**

THE DRIFT SERIES

Double Down

All in

Wild Card

Three of a Kind

No Limit